Praise for Teresa LaBella and Danger Reveal

"A brilliant read that will keep you captivated beginning to end!" — **Florence Mazerolle, Author of the *In Four Languages* series, and recipient of the Queen Elizabeth II Platinum Jubilee medal**

"The book kept me guessing throughout, a true sign of a well-written suspense. The love scenes weren't bad, either!" —**Angela Campbell, Director, Rock Island Public Library**

"An unputdownable thrill ride!" —**Debbie Whittall, Canadian Writer**

"Delving into the world of human trafficking, *Danger Revealed* brings the reader into the world of those embroiled in it, those trying to stop it, and those trying to get their loved ones back from the brink of the terror that surrounds it." —**Kim Sigafus, Award-winning Native American Author and Speaker**

"Teresa LaBella pulls off a great escape with this brisk blend of intrigue, passion, and thrills." —**Misty Urban, Author of *My Day As Regan Forrester***

"What more would you want in a novel? *Danger Revealed* has it all: international intrigue, private investigators hunting for a kidnapped girl, police trying to bring down a criminal ring, a crime boss that you love to hate, a car chase that makes you want to duck when the bullets start flying, and a bit of romance that allows the characters to become very real for the reader. Teresa LaBella masterfully crafts intrigue, drama, crime and romance into the five-star tale." —**M.L. Williams, author of *The Carly Dilemma* and *Cornfield Chronicles***

More Books by Teresa LaBella

Romance – New Life in Love series

Reservations

Heartland

Belonging

Tales from Heartland

Love Unlikely (novella)

Romantic Suspense

Danger Noted

Political Thriller

Capital Strings

Danger Revealed

Danger Revealed

Teresa LaBella

PURPLE PORCUPINE
PUBLISHING

First Edition

For John

Wherever we may find each other again

TABLE OF CONTENTS

Chapter 1

The Unfulfilled Promise

The open hallway door to the stairway escape slammed closed. The lump of cash dropped with a thump on a wooden desktop marred by letter openers and the occasional stray bullet.

The sharpened tip of a pencil scratching on lined ledger sheets ceased. Rayen Vasquez, an involuntary recruit in a cesspool of crime and wasted lives, squinted dark eyes at the green bundle.

"Tonight's take. Five thousand dollars." Cracked lips ringed by bristles stained yellow from nicotine, formed words Rayen knew were a lie.

The wiry man with a face scarred by acne, fists, and knife blades leaned over Rayen's shoulder. His staccato snorts of sour breath fouled a space too small to absorb the tension. "Tell me!" he ordered her.

Bastardo! Rayen silently cursed the boss who owned her. She reached for the wad of folded bills pinched by a thin red rubber band. Her fingers with nails chewed to raw skin crescents released and ruffled the bills. "Four thousand three hundred fifty," she said.

The courier of stolen cash raised his lips in a snarl. "You gonna believe this lyin' bitch!" He backed away and pivoted on the heels of shoes with untied laces. "I'm outta here."

The wiry man's shrill whistle alerted others who followed his orders. The open hallway door to the stairway escape slammed closed. Rayen's keeper snatched the unbound pile from her. His quick count confirmed her quoted total. His pockmarked cheeks flushed red. "You're the liar, you cheating son-of-a-bitch!"

A glint of metal flashed in the glare of the naked incandescent bulb overhead. Rayen crawled under the desk and tucked into her familiar refuge. She covered her ears. Her lips moved in silent prayer. The crack of gunfire ended another transaction, number seventy-four by Rayen's count. The Bastardo had never let a liar live in the six years, two months and thirteen days she'd been held captive with no passport, no identity, and no way out.

***

Rayen Vasquez had fine-tuned her natural talent to rapidly tally the trinkets sold in the markets of Buenos Aires. Curious tourists bought in to her hustle with pesos from purses and pockets by guessing the number of magazines in a stack at Feria de Libros or costumed doll miniatures in a shop window at San Telmo. How many polished stones were in a vase at Caminito in La Boca or earrings in the jewelry box at a stall in Feria de Plaza Serrano. Anything on display was fair game.

Her unique ability had attracted the attention of a burly man seated on the bar stool next to her at a rundown diner in East St. Louis. The small glass of milk she'd bought with coins found in sidewalk cracks and empty parking lots was almost gone. Her stomach gurgled and growled. The burly man glanced at the daily special noted in black block letters on a whiteboard hanging near the front door and pointed to a sign on the counter. It read: Free lunch!

"What's the catch?" he'd asked the cook flipping burgers on a grill permanently crusted by years of grease.

The hunched-over cook with a turkey neck and skin that sagged where muscle once was, flattened patties of raw meat under a steel spatula. "Guess how many coins are in the jar next to the cash register," he'd said without turning around.

The bar stool squeaked with the swivel. "Nobody can do that," the man on the red padded seat had grumbled.

"I can," Rayen had said and whispered the answer in his ear. He'd shouted the correct number, then filled her belly with the hot beef sandwich lunch special he'd won.

"You from here?" he'd asked her between mouthfuls of coffee from a chipped white cup.

Rayen hadn't eaten a meal since she'd spent the last of the cash her mother had saved to get her out of Argentina. She'd stuffed her cheeks with bread-soaked gravy and could only shake her head in reply.

"Going anywhere in particular?" He'd waited for her answer.

She'd swallowed and swiped a paper napkin over her lips. "Just away from where I was."

He'd finished his coffee. "I'm headed for Chicago. Want a lift?"

She'd hesitated. Something about this rather ordinary man didn't feel quite right. But the driver she'd met over a plate of food seemed a safer option than hitching a ride with a total stranger. He'd guessed her illegal status and urgent need for cash an hour into the Interstate 55 drive north and east across Illinois. "I know a guy who could use you. He'll pay under the table; no questions asked," he'd said.

***

Used was what she'd been—paid enough to live but not enough to leave. She was a link in the chain of the desperate, exploited by human traffickers.

"Haul that garbage out of here!" the scar-faced boss shouted to another of the captured hopeless. "Search him. Strip him if you have to! I want all that money. You!" Strong hands reached under the desk. The brute force pressure of his curled fists bruised her thin arms. She scrambled to her feet and struggled to stand. "Count it. All of it. Write it down."

Rayen focused on the piles of cash and the ledger sheets to block out the blood and whatever the fired bullet had blown out. She couldn't afford to vomit lunch and dreaded the dry heave retch when forced to clean it up.

The mindless task freed her to rekindle the glimmer of hope in a promise unfulfilled that seemed so far out of reach. The image and emotions bonded to the memory of that promise transported Rayen back to daybreak on a street in La Boca, lined by once cheery painted facades faded by time and neglect. Her mother's beauty and spirit were battered, pounded into submission by cruel words and blows. Hidden truth revealed. Money pressed into Rayen's palm. Prayers for a safe journey recited together.

Rayen's vision blurred. Tears fell. Her fingers brushed at the dampness on the ledger sheet's smudged columns of numbers. The ruined and the lost had no names.

Chapter 2

Missing

Kelly turned the key in the lock on the second-floor office door and glanced at the Fitbit on her wrist—8:59 a.m. She sighed and thought out loud. *How is it that we leave home at the same time every morning, and he's always late?* With her hands full of takeout coffee and a clutch purse, Kelly kicked at the door with the heel of her shoe. She dashed to her desk to save her fingers from the heat and cursed the thin sleeve on the poorly insulated disposable cup.

"Hi. Hello?" A woman's voice echoed from the hallway.

Kelly turned back toward the half-open office door. "Yes? Can I help you?"

The door opened a bit wider. "I'm looking for The UnMatchables private detective agency. Have I found it?"

"You have. Come on in." Kelly circled the desk and stowed her purse in the right-hand side bottom drawer.

An abundance of nervous energy stepped through the doorway. She plucked at the pearl buttons on her sea-green suit coat and shifted her weight between feet in shiny black patent leather Mary Jane pumps. "Hi, I'm Tori Deane."

"Kelly Gillespie. Please." Kelly motioned and moved a dozen steps away toward a corner area furnished for meetings. The partners had added a second brown faux leather chair to the space since move-in day nearly a year ago. Light from the golden glass globe shade at the tip of the thin metal neck floor lamp that Eddie referred to as 'the noose' cast a warm glow over the two-cushion couch and matching chairs around a mahogany coffee table. "Make yourself comfortable."

"Thank you." Tori settled and then squirmed in the chair nearest the office door. Long slender fingers twisted the curl at the ends of her shoulder-length ginger-red hair. "I'm embarrassed to be here."

"Don't be." Kelly stepped around the narrow knee-high table between them, tucked the hem of her dress behind her knees, and sat on the edge of the couch cushion.

"I can't tell you how many times I've taken the Edens toward Lake Bluff and turned around at Highland Park." Tori jumped at the sound of footsteps made by hard-soled shoes across the bare oak floor behind her.

"Hey, Kel." Eddie combed his fingers through sandy-brown hair tossed by an expressway drive from Chicago's Loop to the north shore suburb. "No coat and short sleeves. What an incredible day for November! Not a cloud in the sky, and it's gotta be close to seventy. I had to take the lid off Petula." That's when he noticed his partner's forced smile and the heads-up glare in her eyes.

"Petula is his MGB convertible." Kelly nodded toward the woman in the chair. "Can I get you anything? A bottle of water? I think we have some soda in the fridge."

"Thanks, I'm fine." Tori rubbed her forehead. Her hand trembled. "No, I'm not fine. I'm a nervous wreck. I'm sorry. Did I forget to close the door?"

"It's OK." Kelly motioned for Eddie to sit beside her. "Tori, this is my partner."

He offered her his hand. "Eddie Emerson."

"Tori Deane." She wiped her hand on her pencil skirt and shook his. "I've never done anything like this before."

"Most people who come to us haven't." He sat back on the cushion next to Kelly. "So, what did I miss?"

"We were just getting started when you walked in," Kelly said.

Tori glanced over her shoulder and scooted forward in the chair. "Maybe this isn't such a good idea after all." The red leather handbag she clutched opened with her nervous click of the snap that kept it closed. Its contents spilled on the floor at her feet. Kelly helped her collect a cell phone, cosmetics, keys, and the variety of loose paraphernalia that multiplies in a woman's purse. "I'm not usually this clumsy," Tori protested.

"I am," Kelly said. "When I'm nervous, things break." Her attempt to calm their client paid off. Tori sighed and sat back in the chair. "The consultation is on us, and anything you say stays between us. You wouldn't be here unless the reason you sought us out were important."

"You're right." Tori's shoulders slumped. "Of course, you're right. Maybe that water would be nice."

"I'll get it." Eddie brought back a bottle from the mini fridge against the wall near Kelly's desk. He twisted off the cap and handed it to Tori. "Take your time and start from the top." He settled again on the couch beside Kelly.

She took a sip and a breath. "I work at the Art Institute of Chicago. I love my job. I knew that's where I wanted to work from the first time I walked up the steps past the iron lions. I was on a fourth-grade class field trip. I begged my parents to bring me back the next weekend. I spent hours in the galleries just staring at the Van Goghs, the Monets, and the O'Keeffes. I saved my allowance and babysitting money so I could take classes. I was never very good at art, but I didn't care. I just wanted to be there. But that's not what I'm here to talk about." Water squirted from the neck of the bottle, with the plastic crackle of her death grip squeezes. The shower drops of liquid spotted her skirt a darker shade.

"The Art Institute opened a major Canadian exhibit last fall, everything from paintings by the Group of Seven to these glorious sculptures by Inuit artists. We hosted a fundraising gala the night before the exhibit opened to the public—a real schmooze-fest of VIP guests, major donors, and sponsors. You get the picture. Anyway, someone in the crowd bumped my elbow, and I spilled a glass of champagne on the most gorgeous man I'd ever laid eyes on, who happened to be from the office of the Canadian consulate general. I was mortified. I just stood there babbling nonsense about how the Art Institute would pay to clean his clothes. He took my empty glass and asked a waiter for another. His accent was clearly not Canadian. More like from somewhere in Latin America. Sultry and sexy. His smile was more than just friendly. It was …"

"Mischievous?" Kelly prompted.

"Yes! The sort of mischief that tempts you to eat the double chocolate cake you've sworn off until you've lost twenty pounds. You know what I mean?"

Kelly nodded. "I don't know a woman who wouldn't."

"We read each other's name tags. Lucas asked if I would tour the exhibit with him. 'Will you do me the honor, Victoria?' he said. I tell you, little Icky Vickie from Libertyville felt like a princess who'd just found her Prince Charming! The exhibit was on loan from the Art Gallery of Ontario, so the signage was printed in English and French. I felt my knees go weak every time he helped me with my rusty garden variety high school and freshman year college French, most of which I'd forgotten. He asked me who my favorite artist was. I babbled on about Monet haystacks and water lilies. The next day, this enormous bouquet of pink lilies and red roses shows up at the Art Institute with my name on it! His business card was in the envelope with the card that read 'Thank you for the tour. I'd very much like to see you again, Lucas.' I took that as an invitation to call him."

Kelly edged forward on the cushion. "And you did."

"You better believe it! We went to dinner that night. I was so nervous and excited I couldn't eat. But I did drink a bit too much wine. Lucas was a perfect gentleman. He ordered black coffee to sober me up, then took me home and walked me to my front door. I invited him in, but he turned me down. I don't know; maybe he noticed how disappointed I was. He kissed me, sweet and soft at first, then ..." she shivered at the memory. "I swear that kiss set my body on fire!" Tori leaned a shoulder toward Kelly in a conspiratorial 'just between us' gesture. "Oh, the dreams I had that night. I threw my pillow at the alarm clock. I didn't want to wake up." Tori's green-eyed gaze drifted away. She sighed through the smile on her lips. "He didn't turn me down after our next date. That night the dreams were real!"

"He rocked your world!" Kelly said.

"And permanently curled up my toes!"

"Excuse me," Eddie interrupted, "but does the plot of this romance novel have a conflict?"

Tori blinked. "Oh, sorry. I digressed again. Six months ago, Lucas told me he'd be returning to work in Ottawa and his home in Montreal before the summer. He said he tried to refuse the Chicago post but didn't explain why. He just doesn't feel comfortable here. He's thinking about retiring from civil service when he gets back and running for a seat in provincial parliament or maybe even the federal government. That's when I decided to apply for permanent residency in Canada. He was surprised when I told him, but he seemed pleased. He said he wanted us to be together but would never expect me to leave my job, home, and country unless I wanted that, too." She drank from the bottle. The rhythmic pop and crackle continued. "That's when things started running, not so hot."

"Finally," Eddie grumbled. Kelly poked the calf of his leg with the toe of her loafer.

"He says he loves me, and I believe him. Or maybe I've talked myself into believing him. I'm thirty-nine years old. I've heard all the wild stories and statistics about the higher probabilities of being killed by a falling asteroid or a herd of stampeding cattle than finding a husband at my age. I stayed home in my pajamas and watched a movie with my mom on high school prom nights. I made up excuses after six years on two college campuses and no engagement ring on my finger. I wasted seven years with an actor who left for California and eight years with another jerk who promised to marry me as soon as his widowed father died. He eloped with my best friend the day after the funeral." Tori frowned with her finger air quotes around the words 'best friend'. "I'm sorry." Tori dabbed at the corners of her eyes with her fingertips. "I don't mean to ramble on so."

Eddie brushed the spot on his khakis where Kelly had made her point. "At the risk of asking an open-ended question, why exactly do you need a private investigator?"

Tori's lower lip trembled. "I haven't seen or heard from Lucas in two weeks! I call, and I leave messages. I've gone to his office at Two Pru Plaza, and all they'll tell me is he's away on personal business."

"Could he have gone back to Canada early?" Kelly asked.

"And not tell me? Not even say goodbye?" Tori swiped the back of her hand under her nose. "The voicemail messages on his phone at work and his cell phone haven't changed. I'm afraid something has happened to him. I thought about calling the police. But they'd probably think I'm just some jilted girlfriend."

Kelly walked to her desk, slid the top drawer open, and grabbed a box of tissues. *Maybe she is, and maybe she isn't,* Kelly thought. *But if I were in her shoes, I'd sure as hell want some answers.* Kelly brought the box to Tori. "Thank you." She plucked out a wad of tissues and blew her nose.

"Tell us what you know about Lucas," Eddie said, "everything he's told you. Do you mind if we record the interview?"

Tori shook her head. "No, not at all."

Eddie retrieved a digital voice recorder from his desk drawer and set the device on the coffee table. "Let's start over. You mentioned he's from Montreal, but I don't think you've told us his full name."

More tears fell with the effort and embarrassment evident on Tori's face and in her voice. "No, I guess I didn't. His name is Lucas Dominguez, and now that I think about it, I really don't know much about him. He likes his steak rare and prefers red wine. He's fluent in English and French, obviously, and in Spanish. I asked him once if he was born in Canada. He said no that he is Canadian by choice. That's it."

"Did you ever ask him about his, well, his family?" Kelly asked.

"You mean, did I ask if he was or had ever been married?"

"I was trying to be delicate." *As delicate as I can be, considering how much you're willing to give up when he isn't.*

"I know, and I appreciate that. Lucas told me he was married. His wife died of cancer about five years ago. He said they didn't have any children. Last summer, over the Fourth of July weekend, we went to my brother's house in Rosemont for a family cookout. Lucas seemed to have a good time. He played soccer with my brother and nephews. We were all impressed at how good he was at the game. But there was this sadness about him that lasted through the next morning. I felt it even while we were making love. I asked him what was wrong. He wouldn't tell me. He just said that was a long time ago and a world away."

"Have you visited Canada with him?" Eddie asked.

Tori shook her head. "No. He said if he went back home, he wasn't sure he could force himself to come back to Chicago. That's why I'm certain he didn't just leave. Even though he didn't want to be here, he felt obligated to stay until his term in the consulate general's office was over. He loves his country. And I know he loves me as much as I love him." The plea in her red-rimmed eyes mirrored the pain in her voice. "Will you help me find him?"

Eddie clicked off the recorder and cleared his throat. "Well, I'm not sure that..."

Kelly reached across the low table and took Tori's hand. Kelly nudged Eddie's knee with hers. "Of course, we will."

An audible exhale of relief relaxed the tension in Tori's shoulders. "Thank you. You don't know what this means to me. I ..." The cell phone in her purse beeped and repeated four quick alarm bursts. "Oh, my gosh! It's after ten! I've got to get to work." Her attempt to stand and quiet the phone dumped the red bag's contents again. Eddie moved the couch to round up three tubes of lipstick and a pair of ballpoint pens.

"We'll be in touch." Kelly closed the office door in the wake of their new client's chaotic departure. She turned over the business card Tori had handed her and frowned. "She didn't write down her personal cell number. I guess I'll have to call the Art Institute and ask her for it."

"What a flake." Eddie dropped the nearly full water bottle into the recycle bin and sat at his desk. He leaned back in the chair and drummed his fingers on the arms. "Why are we taking this case?"

"Because she needs our help."

"Help with what? Taking a chunk out of her bank account?"

Kelly strode across the hardwood and stood at Eddie's desk. She faced him. Hands on her hips. "What's your problem, Eddie?"

"While I'm all good with making an honest living, this isn't honest. I mean, c'mon, Kel. The guy has obviously dumped her."

"How can you be so sure of that?"

"I sure as hell wouldn't want to be with her."

"I would hope not since you're engaged to me. But that's beside the point and not your call." Kelly paced around her desk and plopped in the chair behind it. "From where I sit, Tori has got a lot going for her. She's got a career she enjoys and family here. But she loves Lucas so much that she's willing to give all that up to be with him. I think it's very romantic."

"I think it's very one-sided."

"So, what are you saying? That we go back on our word and not help her?"

"We'll do some leg work. But I don't think this case is worth spending a whole lot of our time on and running up a big tab she probably can't afford. Maybe this guy feels guilty for leading her on. Maybe he got nervous when she told him she'd applied for permanent residency in Canada. This south of the border fling got too real, and he's trying to let her down easy."

"Or maybe he really is in trouble." Kelly swiveled in the chair and coaxed her computer to life. The monitor flickered. She grabbed her cup of cooled coffee and frowned at the first sip. "Dammit!"

Eddie grinned. "Microwave warm-up or fresh brew?"

"Either or both would be much appreciated." She kissed him as he bent to pick up the takeaway cup from her desk. "Thank you, love," she said. Rich blend aromas followed the beep and whir sounds from the microwave and belched puffs of coffee maker steam. Kelly breathed in the scents of anticipation. *Ah, caffeine. Fuel for the mind and fingers.* She rubbed her palms together. "Now let's see what we can find out about Lucas Dominguez from Montreal."

"What about the Klineberger case?" Eddie ruffled the short stack of file folders filling his inbox. "And the other clients we owe updates and reports?"

"They can wait." Kelly's fingers worked her keyboard. Eye strain prompted the reach in her purse for glasses to scan and read a screen. Mouse clicks between sips from cups of coffee Eddie poured for them, retrieved desired information.

An hour-long search connected some of the pieces of a life puzzle. She leaned back in her chair, massaging the knotted muscle in her neck. Breath held, she blew out a single word through her lips. "Whoa."

"What did you find out?" Eddie rolled in his desk chair to stop alongside hers.

"I sure hope Lucas didn't return to Argentina because if he did, odds are he may not get out."

"Why not? And why would he go to Argentina?"

"Because that's where he was born." Kelly turned her computer monitor to share the information displayed.

Eddie's gaze scanned the page. "So, he's an immigrant. Tori said he chose Canada."

"I don't think choice is an accurate description. He's more like a refugee. Lucas and his family left Argentina about a year after the government was overthrown. His father was a member of the trade unions targeted by the military as dissidents. Javier Dominguez was arrested and tortured. But he was one of the lucky ones. He got out alive. Trade unionists accounted for over half of the Dirty War victims."

"When was this?"

Kelly clicked on the next tab. "The military junta was in power from March 1976 to October 1983. According to the dates in his profile, Lucas was about six or seven years old when he and his family settled in Quebec."

"I remember my dad talking about how much money he and his British clients raked in around that time."

Kelly nodded. "The Falklands War brought down the junta and restored free elections in Argentina. Smart investments probably made them a fortune."

"The plot of this story could feed the novel my publisher has been bugging me to write. Easy to do the research on this true crime. All I'd have to do is

12

interview the second generation." Eddie covered his mouth with his hand. "I think I'm going to be sick."

"I'm not thrilled about where or how your family made more money, either. But what's done is done. There's another reason to help Tori find Lucas."

"Yeah, about that. Why would he go back to Argentina? And why would he be in danger now if he did? All of this happened over forty years ago."

"I'm not sure why he would go back. Maybe his government sent him there on a diplomatic mission."

"Then why would they tell Tori he was away on personal business?"

"Could be the standard response. Like name, rank, and serial number." Kelly clicked on the next tab. "Lucas Dominguez is a senior officer and diplomat, second only to the Consulate General. He also has attaché status."

"Which means?"

"Which means his fluency in multiple languages makes him a very valuable asset to the government of Canada."

"Tori said he's fluent in English, French, and Spanish."

"Add German, Italian, and an indigenous language Inuktitut to that checklist. Here's the problem." A final mouse click opened the state department tab. "Travel alerts from the U.S. Bureau of Consular Affairs warn of an increase in the number of kidnappings in Argentina. Over ninety percent of the crimes were reported in Buenos Aires and surrounding areas. Diplomatic credentials would attract the attention of kidnappers. A foreign diplomat from a first-world country who is also an Argentine national could put a big dollar ransom target on his back."

"The Canadian government would know that. Why risk sending Lucas?"

"They probably wouldn't. My guess is his reason for taking that risk is more personal than business."

Eddie scratched his head. "Then I guess we dig into his past, Watson. Uncover that personal reason."

Kelly grinned at the nickname he assigned her on day one of The UnMatchables. Who knew her rescue of alcoholic Eddie from a South Side bar would spark a career change and new life in love with her best friend since college. "So, the game begins, Sherlock."

Chapter 3

First Clues

O ver the next few days, the PI partners worked a sketchy plan and walked through a shallow pool of possible leads.

Eddie delivered a grande cup of takeaway coffee to the station house where his friend Detective Jim Ross was on early shift duty. As a reporter for the Chicago Tribune, Eddie had walked these halls, gathered facts, and soaked up research that fed the plots for his true crime novels. Jim had been the investigating officer on many of the criminal cases covered, stories printed or streamed on newsfeeds under Eddie's byline. The veteran detective read and red-lined Eddie's manuscripts "for belly laughs" and then fed the author facts from closed case files for the next book in the series.

Jim peeled the lid off the cup with a logo recognizable to locals and gulped the steaming contents.

"For the life of me, I don't know how you can do that." Eddie sat in the break room chair across from Jim. One leg was shorter than the others and caused the wooden table between them to tilt slightly to the left.

"I'll tell you what I say to my partner," Jim said in reference to junior detective in age and seniority only, Paul Callaway. "Years of pain and practice, buddy. But I know you didn't come here to keep me caffeinated. What's this about?"

"I need some advice about a case."

Jim sat back and crossed his ankle over his knee. "Huh." He rubbed the stubble on his chin. "In over your head?"

"I don't even know where to jump in. The guy Kelly and I are looking for is a Canadian diplomat in the consular general's office."

"Who's asking? Never mind." Jim reached for his coffee. "I know what you're going to say—client confidentiality. But I also know it sure as hell isn't the Canadian government. They keep close tabs on their people. Even in the worst-case scenario, a body in the morgue would be out of here before rigor mortis sets in."

"I figured that."

"You can try the direct route and ask the consulate where this guy is. But they probably won't tell you."

"Our client already did, and they didn't."

"I'm guessing due to the nature of your love 'em or leave 'em beast that your client is a friend missing the benefits." Jim snorted. "Open and shut case, and thank you very much for your business. Easy work if you can get it."

"I'll admit that was my gut reaction. I didn't want to take the case or her money. But Kelly insisted." Eddie leaned over the table. "C'mon, Jim. Help me out here. If this were your case, where would you start?"

Jim traced the thick pad of his index fingertip around the rim of the paper cup. "I'd ask around. Go to every watering hole, storefront, and park bench in between Two Pru and where he lives. Somebody has seen or heard something."

Eddie sucked in a breath and let it out in a low whistle. "That's a lot of ground to cover."

"Welcome to my world." Jim slurped the rest of his coffee. "Look. Forget about Two Pru. This guy probably blends in with every other suit on any given day."

Ya think? Tell me something I don't know. "Can we skip the process of elimination?"

Jim laughed. "OK, hotshot. Start where he lives. Ask the super. Did he move out? Is his car still there? If this guy's been living there for a while, somebody got used to seeing him around. Ask his neighbors. They might be able to tell you when and how he left. Was he in a hurry? Was he alone? Did he leave with somebody? Was he carrying more than a briefcase?"

Eddie nudged Jim's empty cup. "And what if I come up empty?"

Jim stuffed the lid in the cup and tossed it in a nearby waste basket. "You won't."

***

Autumn's golden light warmed the air, cooled by an occasional breeze. The earthy odor of decaying leaves lifted with the blown grit and dust.

Kelly sneezed. "Ugh! I almost wish it would snow." She stood beside Eddie at the T-junction of the sidewalk around the parking lot and to the front doors of the apartment building where Lucas lived. Mostly bare branches of knee-high bushes planted on either side of the cement trembled in a sudden gust of wind.

Eddie zipped up his jacket. "You'll get your wish soon enough." He glanced at the cell phone in his hand.

"Anything?" Kelly asked.

"Nope. Not a text message or a call." He scrolled through his contact list, tapped the building superintendent's cell phone number, and frowned. "Voicemail."

Kelly shivered and flipped up the collar of her coat. "I guess he doesn't want to talk to us."

"Well," Eddie said and looked around, "let's split up and find someone who does."

Eddie circled the building. A long-legged jogger approached. "Excuse me," Eddie called out to her. She rushed past without pausing for a question that would break her ponytail-swing steady stride.

Kelly walked the path around the parking lot. A gray-suited man tossed his briefcase through an opened car door. "Hi. Hello," Kelly began. He glanced at the image of Lucas she'd downloaded to her cell phone. "Sorry. Don't know him," he said as he slid behind the steering wheel and slammed the door closed.

"This place is a fortress." Eddie met up with Kelly in the vacated spot reserved for tenant number thirty-two's car. "Closed circuit cameras, key code entry, and wireless alarm systems everywhere. It's almost as secure as our penthouse."

"That makes foul play a less than likely explanation." She looked around at the empty sidewalks and green space leading up to and surrounding the buildings and sighed. "I guess our work here is done."

"Excuse me, miss." An elderly woman crossed from the parking lot behind Kelly and stood at her shoulder. Imitation red glass jewels on the gold collar of the white teacup poodle in her arms sparkled in the fading rays of reflected sunlight. "Are you looking for someone?"

"Yes." Kelly held out her cell phone. "Have you seen him?"

"Not for a while." She pointed to a slate blue four-door sedan parked two stalls to her right. "That's his car." She smiled at Kelly. "He lives in my building. He's a very nice man. He always helps me with my groceries. Very polite. Lovely accent." She winked. "Nice-looking, too."

"Do you remember the last time you saw him?" Eddie asked her.

She wrinkled her nose and pressed her lips together. "Two, maybe three weeks ago. He left in a cab late in the afternoon or early evening, as I recall. I was waiting for my ride to go to church. So, it must have been a Wednesday. He had a suitcase, one of those bags on wheels with a pull-up handle. He seemed to be in a hurry. And he looked worried. Or scared. I couldn't really tell which." Watery blue eyes behind cats-eye designer-frame glasses with rhinestones at the temple points stared back at Kelly. "I hope he's not in some kind of trouble."

"That's what we hope to find out." Eddie offered her his arm. "May we walk you to your door?"

Her smile widened. "That would be nice." She linked her arm through his. "What a nice young man you are. My name is Ruby."

"Glad to make your acquaintance, Ruby. I'm Eddie. This is my fiancée, Kelly."

"Congratulations. When's the wedding?"

Eddie glanced at Kelly and smiled at Ruby. "That's a question that hasn't been answered yet."

Kelly scowled back at him. *Really, Eddie? That's the best comeback you've got?* "We haven't set a date yet."

"Well, don't wait too long. I was married to my Henry for fifty-two years. That time passed so quickly. We thought we had forever. Then he was gone. I've been alone now for ten years. Doesn't seem possible." She stopped at the locked outer door. Kelly checked the tenant list as Ruby punched in the key code. The lock clicked. Eddie opened the metal-framed glass door.

17

"Lucas lives in apartment 252," she whispered in his ear.

Eddie stepped through the door with Ruby on his arm and petted her fidgety dog with his free hand. The pup licked his thumb.

"Cosmo seems to like you. Do you have a dog?"

"Not yet," Eddie replied.

What do you mean, not yet? Kelly's frown deepened. *Not ever!*

"Take my advice. After you're married, but before you start a family, get a fur baby, preferably a puppy. It helps you get used to caring for that little one in the middle of the night." Ruby hugged Cosmo and kissed the fur between his ears. "My Henry and I had two sons. I don't know what I'd do without Michael and Danny." She winked at Kelly. "Babies are worth every minute of lost sleep."

Kelly held back her anger until Ruby was securely in her first-floor apartment. "What the hell was that all about?" Her lowered voice hissed past her teeth. "It's none of her business when we'll get married, if we have a dog, or how soon, or even if we'll have kids."

Eddie frowned at her. "Lighten up, Kel. She's an older lady making polite conversation."

"You could have changed the subject."

"You could stop putting me off and agree to set a date." He crossed to the other side of the hallway and motioned for her to join him.

"And what's this about a dog?" Kelly stood her ground and folded her arms over her chest. "You've never said anything about getting a dog."

"We'll talk about this later," Eddie responded in a tone above a whisper. He pressed his finger to his lips. "Get behind me and follow my steps."

"Why?"

"Why do you have to ask the obvious?" He nodded to points in overhead corners. "To keep out of camera view."

Eddie took the lead down the carpeted hallway and stairs that led to the second-floor hallway. He pressed his ear against the solid door below the brass number 252.

"Now what, Sherlock?"

Eddie glanced to his left and right. "We gain entry."

"We're breaking in?"

"No, we're investigating." Eddie eyed the keypad mounted above the brass door handle.

"I hope you don't expect me to do that," Kelly whispered. "I pick locks. I don't do keypads."

"Reason being?"

"Because the possibility of alarms going off makes me nervous."

Eddie's eyebrows rose. "Now you tell me." He punched in a series of numbers. The keypad flashed green. The lock clicked open.

"How did you do that?" Kelly asked.

"Elementary, my dear Watson. I watched Ruby. It's a simple combination—the building number followed by the apartment and floor numbers. Let's hope the same combination turns off the internal alarm. Wait here." Eddie slipped through the half-open door. He returned within seconds and held it open for Kelly. "Looks like Lucas left in such a rush he forgot to set the alarm."

"Apparently." Kelly scoped out the trail of discarded clothing and unwashed dishes stacked in the kitchen sink. The dining area with built-in cupboards and shelves had been converted into a home office. "That's odd. He also left his computer." Kelly sat at the desk and opened the laptop on it. "Maybe he forgot to do something else." A quick move of the mouse flashed a disappointing message on the screen. "Dammit."

"What now?"

"Well, of course, it's locked and protected by passcode."

"That doesn't usually stop you."

"Not if I have time, which I don't. I can't take this with me. That would be grand theft and could start an international incident." She pointed at the red maple leaf icon displayed on the screen.

Eddie spied a notepad and pencil next to the laptop. "Maybe what we're looking for isn't on the computer. Observe." His back-and-forth brush of the pencil over letters and numbers pressed into the paper spelled out a message and a clue.

"Flight 750. Leaves O'Hare 9:45 p.m. Arrives Buenos Aires 8:45 a.m."

The PIs eyed each other.

"This isn't good." Eddie dropped the pencil and pondered what to tell Tori. "Watson, I'm willing to bet Lucas is in Argentina."

Kelly reread the uncovered message. "Oh shit, Sherlock. Do we tell Tori what we know and how we know it?" Kelly closed the laptop.

Chapter 4

Disclosure

Tori ended the day as she had every day since she'd hired The UnMatchables to find Lucas. She let Cassie out to pee on the tiny patch of urban grass outside the back door of her ground-floor apartment. She brushed her teeth, put on pajamas, and called Kelly.

"Anything?" Tori would ask.

"I'm afraid not. But we're not out of ideas or leads yet. Don't give up hope."

Hope was all Tori had to hold on to. She breathed a silent sigh of relief at the end of the nightly news broadcast, then braced for the iron grip return of anxiety. She'd reluctantly washed her bed sheets but couldn't strip off the case over the pillow where his faint scent lingered. The ears of the dog curled up at her feet perked up when Tori began her nightly run-down description of her day with the absent Lucas. She told him about the silent auction winner that called to complain about the all-expenses-paid Caribbean cruise package with coach-class airline tickets when he and his guest expected to fly first class. She bragged about the six-figure major gift she'd secured from a donor with a history of giving the Art Institute a consistent five thousand dollars in December. She begged him to call and let her know where he was and that he was safe. She hugged his pillow and told him she loved him in three languages.

Je t'aime. Te quiero. I love you. Tori fell asleep, wishing and praying that he would soon be in her arms again.

Cassie's low growl and high-pitch yip woke Tori in mid-dream of him. "What is it, Cassie?" The dog's paws touched down at the foot of the bed. Her hasty canine skid toward the front door bunched the round throw rug into a lumpy heap.

Tori tossed back the bedclothes and stepped into pink and white fluffy bunny scuffs. She slipped her arms into the robe Cassie had curled into at the foot of the bed. The sleeves were still warm from the Westie terrier mix breed's body.

The bounce and scratch of paws at the front door echoed down the hallway. Tori flipped switches on the wall along the short path to where her dog sniffed at the entryway crack under the door. She squinted into the darkness through the single diamond-shaped window. Someone was standing on the other side. Should she turn on the porch light or call 9-1-1? Tori hesitated.

"Victoria?" His voice, hoarse from illness or fatigue, wavered above a whisper.

"Lucas!" She flipped the lock and opened the door. "Are you really here?" Her arms embraced him to make sure. "Where have you been? I was so afraid something had happened to you. I knew you wouldn't leave without telling me why."

"Oh, mon amour. My beautiful one." He smoothed tangled strands from her forehead and kissed her lips. "I'm so sorry. I couldn't tell you. I couldn't tell anyone where I was going or why I had to go."

Glow from the light inside deepened the dark circles of extreme exhaustion under his eyes. Tori let go of him and grabbed the handle of his suitcase on wheels. "Give me your coat. Sit down before you fall over."

Cassie scampered at his heels from the doorway to the couch. The delighted little dog jumped up in his lap and licked his nose. "Hola, Cassie." Lucas scratched behind her ears. The contented canine circled, settled, and sighed.

Tori locked the door and sat beside him. "Can I get you anything? Are you hungry? Thirsty? You look bone tired."

"This is what I need." His arm around her shoulders gently moved her closer. "Thinking of you, of coming back to you, kept me focused on who I am now and not on where or what I was."

I love who you are. I don't care what you were. You've come back to me. She swallowed the lump rising in her throat. "I don't understand," she whispered.

His finger under her chin turned and tilted her head. The look in eyes she'd longed to see again foreshadowed an admission Tori wasn't sure she was ready to hear. "I returned to a place of such pain. I had no desire to go there again. But I had to know. I had to try. Still, I remain in the dark. I can tell you the beginning. I don't yet know the end." She could feel the sadness in his kiss as his lips brushed hers. "I love you, Victoria, and I want to be with you for the rest of my life. But what I'm about to say may change how you feel about me."

He sank back into the comfort of the cushions. Tori reached for the throw folded over the back of the couch and covered them with the soft fleece imprint likeness of a Monet haystack painting. She snuggled against him and waited for him to speak.

"My past came back to me from a folder in a file cabinet that I hadn't bothered to open in the eighteen months since I've been here. In it was an emergency request for a visa to return to Canada from a woman whose permanent residency status had expired. She wanted to come to Canada with her daughter and granddaughter. The daughter is a Canadian citizen. The granddaughter was born in Argentina. The application had been reviewed and provisionally approved for processing through the consular general's office in Chicago. But the case was marked inactive. The women and the child never left Buenos Aires."

Lucas pressed his thumb and forefinger against closed eyelids. His hand trembled. Tori brushed her fingers across his forehead and softly traced the broad streaks of silver over black at his temples. *He's gone grayer.* "You're so tired, love. Let's go to bed. You can tell me the rest of your story in the morning."

"No. I need to tell you now." He moved closer to her. She rested her head on his chest. He began again. "The memories of my home country are vague and opaque, like looking through the thin fabric of my mother's scarves." The beat of his heart thrummed in rhythm with the vibration of his voice. "I was a child when we fled, so I remember our house larger than it likely was. I remember the dust in the street where my brothers Nicolas and Tomas kicked a ball at each other. At first, I watched. Then I got in the way. They included me in the game when I took the ball away from them."

Tori smiled at the vision imagined by his description of that particular memory.

"The Ruiz family lived in the house across the street. I remember my mother and Camila Ruiz knitting on our front porch for hours. The metal needles clicked in rhythm with the songs that played on the radio." His hand squeezed her shoulder. "I had such a crush on Adriana Ruiz. She was two years older than me. She had long black hair that her mother would braid and tie with red and gold ribbons. Her laugh was musical, like wind chimes."

"I remember the day my father didn't come home from work." Tori felt his arm around her stiffen ever so slightly. "My mother's friend wept in her arms because her husband also was missing. I remember the flash and thunder of the bomb that leveled our home. My mother's desperate attempt to save us all and her screams when she realized she could not. I remember my father running toward us. The wounds inflicted by his torturers were discolored and bleeding. My fingers were crushed in my mother's hand. My sister Elena clung to our mother and held on as we ran through the remains of all we'd known. Adriana and her mother ran beside us. We all packed in between the open slats of a flatbed truck used to hold and haul products to market. We fled the collapse of our country. We left summer behind and traveled for so long and so far to a cold and snow I'd never seen or felt or even thought possible. Most of the people spoke a language none of us knew. Almost no one spoke Spanish. We lived in two small rooms and shared a washroom with another family. Adriana and I grew up together. We pledged our bodies, lives, and souls to each other. After the war ended, her homesick mother wanted to return to Argentina. Adriana went with her. I wrote to her at the address Camila Ruiz gave to my mother, but my letters were returned unopened."

Tori lifted her head. Lucas had opened his eyes. The pain poured out of them and him. The words he spoke assumed the tone of confession. "The names on the case file in my office are Camila Ruiz and Adriana Vasquez. I went to Argentina to find my first love, her child, and her mother and bring them back home with me to Canada. I failed this time. But you must understand, Victoria. I will keep trying."

Tori tucked the throw around his slumped shoulders. She didn't know what else to do or say. In that rare moment, Tori had lost her words.

Chapter 5

The Evidence

Kelly picked up the cell phone to stop the face-down buzz dance of the device across the table at her side of the bed. The pre-dawn message she'd tried to ignore had gone to voicemail.

"Hi Kelly, it's Tori. I really need to talk to you. Can you call me as soon as you get this? Thanks."

Eddie sandwiched his head between down-filled pillows and moaned. "She is relentless."

"And god-awful early about it." Kelly yawned and rolled into the warmth of him under the fluff of the flannel-covered duvet over them. "So, what are we going to tell her?"

He stuffed both pillows behind his head and kissed Kelly's forehead at the spot where her honey-blonde hair naturally parted. "Until we can confirm where Lucas is without revealing how we got that information, there's nothing to tell."

"We could dig deeper at Two Pru Plaza."

"We've been to the Consulate General's office separately and together. Those lips are sealed."

"Maybe somebody outside that office overheard him making hotel reservations or booking a rental car. He could have been in the lobby or getting a cup of coffee."

"That's a stretch, Kel."

"You got any other ideas?"

"I'm working on it."

"That's my standard daily answer to Tori, and it's getting pretty old."

They groaned at the insistent repeat buzz of the cell phone. "I might as well pick up and get this over with." Kelly held the phone to her ear. "Hi, Tori. Sorry, but I don't have anything new to report on Lucas."

"I do! He's here!"

"Sorry? He did what now?" Kelly nudged Eddie. "Lucas came back," she said and turned the phone's volume up full. "Say again?"

"Lucas is here! He's asleep on my couch. I must have dozed off, too. But I'm wide awake now. I'm so relieved he's safe! I'm so happy!"

"That's great," Kelly replied. *There has to be more to this story.* "Did he tell you where he was and why he left?"

"Yes, and yes. And he needs your help. I'd rather he explain it to both of you. Can you come over and see us today? There's plenty of coffee. Lucas loves my cinnamon crumb cake. Please, Kelly." She lowered her voice. "We're not sure. But who he went to Buenos Aires to find could be right here in Chicago."

"I'll let you know when we're on our way. See you soon." Kelly ended the call.

Eddie sat up and swung his legs over the side of the bed. "That sounds cryptic. Not to mention way out of our wheelhouse."

"How do you mean?" Kelly got out of bed and slipped her arms into the sleeves of a fleece robe.

"The problem Tori hired us to solve is, well, solved. And we don't have to reveal how and what we found out about where Lucas went." Eddie stepped into slippers and headed for the ensuite bathroom. "Missing lover found. Case closed."

"No, it isn't." Kelly followed him across the carpet and onto the bath's terrazzo tile. Sensors in the room detected motion, and the lights turned on. "You heard Tori. There's still a person missing."

Eddie grabbed and wrapped a towel around his waist. "Yeah. A person who may or may not be in Chicago and may or may not want to be found." He scrubbed his palms over a day-old growth of stubble. "And why hire us? Need I remind you Lucas is a Canadian diplomat with high-level access to pull government levers." Eddie peered at his reflection in the mirror over the white marble-topped double sink vanity. "Maybe I'll grow a beard. What do you think, Kel?"

"I think you're changing the subject. Stalling for time. Well, don't bother." Kelly turned on the shower. "I know you. You're as curious as I am, or you would have just rolled over and gone back to sleep." She stripped off her robe and tossed it at him. "You're hard-wired to chase the facts behind the clues. You'll dive into this mystery and ride out every breaking wave until you know the ending." She stepped under jets set for overhead rainfall and gentle pulse massage.

Eddie's chin dropped to his chest in mock defeat. "She knows me better than I know myself," he muttered.

Kelly had dumped bottles of Eddie's addiction down the sink and sponsored the admitted alcoholic through AA. Eddie had bailed her out at the brink of spending addiction bankruptcy. They'd declared love, too long denied on the night they nearly died together. Private investigator partners at the end of their first slam dunk case that could have gone horribly wrong. They survived, consummated, and celebrated their love in the home they now share. Eddie's family owns the posh penthouse on North Lake Shore Drive, the old-money, ultra-affluent Emersons of Fairfield County, Connecticut. He'd proposed, and she'd accepted the ring he'd bought but couldn't give her until he got and stayed sober. The emerald green of her namesake kept through his four soured love affairs and her two failed marriages.

Her scent surrounded him, from shower gel and shampoo to what lingered on the robe in his hands. He breathed deep and vowed to keep their heads above water.

***

The front door opened before the sound of the doorbell chime faded.

"Kelly! Eddie!" Tori greeted her guests. The dog at her feet wriggled and grinned.

"Who's this?" Eddie patted his thigh. "Hey, there, pup!" The dog looked up at Eddie and leaned against his shin.

"That's Cassie," Tori said. "She loves everybody."

"So does my baby sister Cassandra. Mom doesn't like it when I call her Cassie." Eddie bent and gently ruffled tufts of soft fur under the dog's chin. "But my sister prefers her nickname. How about you, Cassie?" The dog yipped in reply.

"Let our guests in, baby girl." The warmth of Tori's cozy apartment chased away the chill they stepped in from. Sunlight through thin white lace curtains on a double-paned window cast delicate patterns on the beige pile carpet. The sweet scent of cinnamon mingled with the aroma of freshly brewed coffee.

Lucas sat at the far end of a white leather couch surrounded by a pair of pine rocking chairs and a hard plastic top table with black metal foldable legs. Round white china plates and mugs, silver knives, forks, and spoons were lined up like soldiers on the table set to serve. The white edges of the Monet fleece blanket around his broad shoulders accentuated the dusting of pale silver in an otherwise black-whiskered full beard. Waves of thick, collar-length hair framed lines and shadows of lingering exhaustion. But the spark of life in his dark eyes projected a determination of spirit fueled by inner strength.

Eddie extended his hand across the table. "I'm Eddie Emerson, and this is my partner… "

"Kelly. Of course." Lucas shook Eddie's hand and smiled at Kelly. "Thank you for being there for Victoria when I was not. I know how difficult this must have been for her."

No, you don't, Kelly thought. *I can read you like a sleazy erotica romance novel. You're the dude on the cover with his shirt and fly open. You are so full of yourself. I know why Tori fell so hard and fast for you, but you can't fool me. I can see what she won't.*

"Coffee and cake as promised." Tori carried a large carafe and a plate of muffins nested in paper baking cups. "Please sit," she said to the PI partners and poured their mugs full. "Super strong, just the way you like it, love," she said and set a mug in front of Lucas. "I'll be right back with milk and sugar."

He sipped the coffee and closed his eyes. A contented sigh passed through his lips. "She looks after me."

"She was worried sick about you," Kelly said. The scowl on her face amplified the anger in her voice. "How could you disappear for weeks? No phone calls. No texts. Not even a note. Then show up at her door and expect to be taken care of and forgiven."

Eddie frowned to mask his shock at her outburst. "We're here to listen, not judge."

"It is a valid question." Lucas looked up and over the rim of the mug. "The answer requires an explanation and examination of the evidence."

"Would anyone like some butter for the muffins?" Tori had returned with a pint-sized silver pitcher and a lidded white china sugar bowl.

"You've done enough, mon amour. Please." Lucas patted the cushion beside him and set the mug back on the table. He grabbed a jacket draped over the arm of the couch. He retrieved a wrinkled, opened envelope from the inside pocket that he handed to Eddie.

"Western Union." Eddie read the penned addresses smudged and blurred by time and handling between international transit points. Contact with sweat, water, or another form of liquid had erased a few of the numbers and letters. "Who is Adriana Vasquez?"

"The past I risked losing my future to find." Lucas stroked Tori's wrist with the tips of his fingers.

"Do you know what was inside?" Eddie asked.

"A money order for 200 U.S. dollars sent by someone in Chicago," Lucas answered.

"I'm not familiar with this local address." Eddie passed the envelope to Kelly.

Kelly felt her heart race even as the chill of recognition made her shiver. *It's down the street from where my brother lost his car, watch, wallet, and life.* "It's a bodega on the South Side." Kelly handed the envelope back to Lucas. "Not a neighborhood to walk around without a loaded weapon or a bodyguard that has one, and definitely not after dark."

The fingers Lucas dragged through his hair trembled. The words he spoke were not in English. He leaned forward, elbows on his knees. The spirit of determination flickered to flame behind his eyes. "I need you to help me find the person who sent that money order. Whoever that is may be able to tell me what happened to Adriana and her daughter. Perhaps lead me to them."

"Why us?" Eddie asked Lucas the question Kelly had avoided. "You have diplomatic immunity and the Canadian government in your corner."

Lucas paused and pressed his palms together. "Diplomatic channels, while effective, are slow. Too slow for what I fear is a life-threatening situation."

"I suppose we could start by asking a detective friend of ours if he knows who to talk to at the South Side station house," Kelly said.

"No!" Lucas shouted. His fingers curled into fists. "No police!"

"Lucas." Tori grasped his hands in both of hers. "If Kelly thinks the police can help …"

He shook his head. "I'm sorry. I was warned not to talk to the police."

"By who?" Eddie asked.

Lucas tossed the envelope on the table between the plate of cakes and the carafe. "You have seen the evidence. The story I have to tell is the explanation. Do you have the time to hear me out?"

Eddie sat back and settled in, his ankle crossed over his knee. "That's what we're here for."

Lucas leaned back and draped the fleece throw around his and Tori's shoulders. "I don't know why I opened that file cabinet drawer. I knew the cases in it were inactive…"

Chapter 6

Buenos Aires

The Argentina he'd known as a boy was gone, changed by forty-two years of recent history. Yet, the memory of what had been remained as real to Lucas as the violet blooms of the jacaranda trees and the beef empanadas on his plate.

The familiar food of his childhood prepared in the restaurant's kitchen and served at an outdoor table on the corner of el Caminito in La Boca did not comfort him. Almost three weeks of long days into his search had revealed nothing. Anyone who could tell him what had happened to Camila Ruiz or might know where to look for Adriana and her daughter averted their eyes and shook their heads. "Lo siento, no lo se. I'm sorry, I don't know." Every night Lucas returned to his hotel room in San Telmo with more questions and no answers.

His plan of anonymity had worked so far. He'd packed no computer. The burner phone in his pocket could not be traced. Lucas presented his Argentine passport at the Chicago O'Hare departure gate and again on arrival at Ezeiza International Airport. He had intended to leave behind all trace of foreign citizenship, then decided at the last minute to take the precaution needed for a safe return. The Canadian passport zippered in his carry-on would guarantee help from the embassy. If he could get there. Lucas refused to consider the sinister circumstances of that dire possibility.

The break he'd thought might never come arrived in the form of a message sealed in a plain white envelope. The hotel desk clerk told Lucas a boy frequently chased away from the front doors had likely been paid to deliver it. "One of the street children that guards parked cars for money," the clerk explained in Spanish. "A man he did not know said the note was for you."

Lucas drank from his glass of Mendoza region Malbec and watched the entwined couple perform the precision steps, kicks, and lunges of tango. The scarlet skirt of the woman in her partner's arms swirled and brushed his table. The contact Lucas was there to meet appeared in the spin of that distraction.

"Senor Dominguez." The well-dressed middle-aged man towered over the table. He righted the chair that leaned against the wall near the open door of the restaurant and sat across from Lucas. "I see you've followed my instructions."

Lucas pushed aside the plate. "I was hungry, and it's too warm to eat inside."

"You've grown used to the cold. Heat in November is uncomfortable for a Canadian." The gemstone in the ring on the third finger of the man's right hand flashed as he raised it to dismiss surprise. "I know who you are. So do others. The questions you ask are dangerous." The man's gray-eyed gaze darted from side to side, sizing up the crowd and movement around them. A quick reach of the ring-weighted hand into his jacket's breast pocket produced a wrinkled and creased envelope, yellowed by exposure to air and sunlight, smudged by semi-legible multi-colored ink markings. "This may help you find what you're looking for."

Lucas unfolded and studied the clue in his hands. "Where did you get this?"

"That is not important. Adriana Ruiz de Vasquez is no longer in Buenos Aires. She sent her daughter away to protect her from her husband's illegal trade. Camila Ruiz is dead. She is at rest in La Chacarita." He leaned across the table. "You have been marked by those who do not wish to be found. Do not ask any more questions or talk to the police here or wherever you return. Listen to me and do as I say." He tapped the table with the tips of his fingers, physical bullet points attached to each instruction. "Get a taxi. Go back to the hotel. Check out. Do not stay the night. Book the first flight you can to where you came from." In a swift tick of seconds, he stood and rounded the corner at el Caminito and was gone.

31

Lucas sat stunned. You have been marked replayed over and again in his mind. The ominous warning relayed by a stranger recalled the scars of torture on his father's body, inflicted by the evil in this land that could never be home again. The scene around him that had seemed so benignly festive minutes ago felt suddenly hostile. He emptied his pocket of pesos to pay for his dinner and called for a taxi. The driver waited for him at a market where he bought a bouquet of flowers with American dollars. Within the hour, Lucas had a confirmed seat on a red-eye flight back to Chicago. He had one last stop and question to ask on the way to the airport.

The driver sat in the idling taxi at the cemetery's entrance. Lucas approached three men with shovels digging a fresh grave. "Disculpe donde puedo encontrar la tumba de Camila Ruiz?" Excuse me, where can I find the grave of Camila Ruiz? A worker using his shovel as a cane walked Lucas down rows of abandoned graves where weeds thrived with bundled dead bouquets.

The bare ground at her grave site slanted slightly from burial edges to center. A simple marker certified her name and the impersonal line from birth to finality. Proof engraved in stone of his failure to save her. Camila Ortega de Ruiz. He whispered the words as an apology, a prayer of blessing, and a promise. Fingertips pressed to his lips touched the cool stone. The scent of fresh flowers faded with his footsteps.

Chapter 7

South Side Chicago

Noises of urban life backfilled the quiet that settled after Lucas relayed and described every detail of his youth and recent past. Tori huddled closer to him, lay her head on his shoulder, and touched the fleece throw to the corners of her eyes.

Eddie cleared his throat. "Well. That's a lot to process and not much to go on."

The combined strain and release of retelling had noticeably drained Lucas. His face paled. His shoulders sagged. "I understand," he said. "You can't help me."

"I didn't say that." Eddie picked up the Western Union envelope. "We have a place to start. Bodegas usually have security cameras. With luck and some persuasion, we'll match up the date this was sent out with the memory of the clerk who made the transaction. The time stamp on the video will link a face with the money."

"That gives me hope." Lucas closed his eyes. "Thank you."

Kelly eased up and out of the rocking chair. "We should go."

"I'll get your coats." Tori wriggled out from under the fleece throw.

Kelly slipped her arms into the jacket she'd hung on the rocking chair's ladder back. Eddie hadn't taken his off.

"Oh. I'm sorry. I should have offered to take your coats," Tori sputtered.

"That's OK, Tori," Kelly said. "Thanks for the coffee. The cake was delicious."

"Thank you for coming to see us on such short notice. And for doing whatever you can for Lucas." Tori hugged them both and scooped Cassie up mid-trot toward the open door.

"Flake," Eddie muttered on the way back to their car.

"Stop saying that," Kelly said. "She's stressed out, she loves him, and her heart is in the right place. He's traveled a rough road, and she's willing to go the distance with him. Call me a diehard romantic, but I believe they can."

Eddie got in behind the wheel of the new white Jeep that had recently replaced Kelly's unreliable high mileage and older model Cherokee. "That's a 180-degree turnaround for you."

"What do you mean?"

"When we arrived, you were ready to throw Lucas under the bus. What was that about?"

She shrugged. "He reminded me of guys I've known like him, that's all."

"Like what?"

"Guys with inflated egos, foreign accents, and what my mother called bedroom eyes."

"Bedroom eyes." Eddie snickered. "That's rich. Who had bedroom eyes?"

"My first ex-husband, that's who!"

"Did I ever meet him?"

"No, you didn't. And you didn't miss much." *Steam with no substance and a short marriage that ran cold in record time. All I got out of it was six months of twice-a-day sex, a miscarriage, and thirty thousand dollars in lost savings and credit card debt.* "I don't want to talk about it or any topic even remotely related to him."

"OK. Forget I asked." Eddie slid the envelope he still held in his hand onto the dashboard. "Where exactly is this bodega?"

On a street, I never want to see again. "It's a long way from North Shore Drive and home, which is where we're going."

"What's your rush?" Eddie turned the key in the ignition. "It wouldn't hurt to get a jump on this case."

A burnt orange brick building with red awnings and bars over the window and door. White lines in the street. Straight lines for walking between the cut curb corners. Curved around the outline of a body. Kelly shivered. "I don't need to go there. I know what it looks like."

34

"Well, I don't." Eddie punched the South Side address into the Jeep's GPS. "Why do you need that?"

"Apparently, you won't tell me where it is, and the address is South Side."

"Don't you think I know that!"

"OK, now what's wrong?"

"It's been a longer than usual day with a too-early start. I'm tired, Eddie. I want to go home."

What is she not telling me? Eddie glanced at the dashboard clock. "We've still got a few hours of daylight left. We'll do a drive-by. Get out. Ask a few questions. You can stay in the car."

"I am not staying in the car alone. Not in that neighborhood."

"Whatever, Kel. Your call." Directions given in a pleasant feminine digital voice were the only words either of them heard for over a half hour. Eddie slotted the Jeep into a tight space against the curb along the street a half dozen city blocks off South Kedzie Avenue.

Wind gusts from a forecasted storm tumbled discarded food wrappers and other escaped disposables down narrow ribbons of pavement. Adults in various stages of age and agility gathered children at the opened door of a school bus in need of bodywork. A young boy in a striped stocking cap and faded jean jacket walked a mostly white pit bull tethered to him by a red leash and harness.

Eddie got out of the car and remotely locked the doors. "This doesn't look that bad."

Not to you. Kelly shoved her hands in her jacket pockets. "Let's get this over with." She crossed the street with him toward the wrought iron-barred door with the red awning. A buzzer inside signaled their entry. The pungent mix of spices, grease, and tobacco made Kelly sneeze. A swarthy-skinned man of unidentifiable years looked up from the Spanish-language newspaper on the counter.

"Hey, good afternoon. I wonder if you can help us." Eddie covered a section of the newsprint with the envelope and smoothed the creases with his palms. "We're trying to find out who sent a money order from here to an address in Buenos Aires about six weeks ago."

The man didn't look at the envelope. "Who's asking?" The hard edges around his South Side Latino accent cut in contrast to the warm, congenial tone Lucas projected. "You cops?"

Kelly cringed.

"No," Eddie answered, "private investigators. Our client is concerned about the welfare of the person whose name is on the money order. Apparently, Western Union couldn't deliver it." Eddie pointed to the security camera anchored to the wall behind and above the bodega clerk's head. "If we could check out the security video, we might be able to match the date stamp with the date the money order was sent from here."

His lip curled. Disgust sprayed with the snort of fine spit between his teeth. "Private dicks." He backhand nudged the envelope off the newspaper. "Camera's broke."

"Is it? Since when?" Eddie reached into his pants' front pocket for his wallet. "How much would it cost to try and fix it?"

"Wouldn't matter. We don't do money orders or Western Union here."

"Really?" Eddie picked up and waved the envelope inches from the clerk's nose. "Then why is your bodega's address on this?"

Thick rubber strips that separated equal sides of metal doors at the back of the store parted with a push from unseen hands. A man of average height but more muscled than the clerk behind the counter stepped through the opening. A once-white apron covered his clothes from shoulders to knees. Stains likely left by remnants of orders prepared for sale from the deli case on the opposite wall smeared the heavy cloth. "Got a problem?" he asked through a mustache as thick as his accent.

Eddie's jaw clenched. The fingers of his right hand balled into a fist. "Not if we can get some cooperation."

"We should go." Kelly took Eddie's arm and backed toward the door.

The clerk's sharp laugh bore the same hard edge as his voice. "Yeah. Better listen to your yegua. Either buy something or get out." The newsprint crinkled with his turn of the page.

Eddie followed Kelly out the door, crossed the street, and let out a long breath on the other side of the closed car door. "Well, that was a waste of your makeup. What's a yegua?"

"I'm not sure. We could ask Lucas."

"It had better be a compliment, or I'll be back to break that guy's nose." He started the car and turned on the heat. "If that cold call was any indicator, I have no idea how we can get any answers without getting the police involved."

Kelly looked away as Eddie steered the car past the spot where her brother's body fell two weeks after his eighteenth birthday. A woman's face emerged in the jagged pain of open-wound memories. The Chicago detective who'd cried with Kelly when every painstaking lead investigated didn't find his killers. The friend who'd turned in her gold shield because a closed case meant failure, and that wasn't an option.

"I do." Kelly thumbed through the contacts on her cell phone. "Call a former cop."

Chapter 8

An Old Friend

Cecily Vosh powered down and closed up her laptop on work she hadn't planned to bring home. "That's enough of that shit for one day." She stretched her arms overhead and cringed at the audible pop reminder of an old shoulder injury from a high-speed chase that ended in a rollover and no arrests.

Bands of black and gray stripes rippled with the stretch of muscles and limbs on the tabby cat in her lap. A soft paw of retracted claws patted Cecily's cheek. "Yeah, I know. It's long past dinner time for both of us, Cornelius." The cat licked his whiskers, and jump-thump landed on the parquet floor.

Cecily filled her companion's ceramic bowl with a scoop of kibble. "There's yours." The cat crouched to feed. "Now for mine." She snorted at the lone rock-hard bag of peas and carrots in the freezer. "Not a pierogi to be found. Dad would be so disappointed." She shuffled packages of ramen noodles and instant soup in cupboards barren of the jerk spice and Jamaican ginger always on hand in her mother's kitchen. "Mama, you'd swear I could not be your child." She opened and closed the fridge door with nearly empty shelves. "Fuck it." Cecily searched the bottom of her purse for her cell phone and ordered a large pepperoni and anchovy pizza delivery.

The cork pulled easily from the last bottle in the six-slot, black metal wine rack on her kitchen counter. "I have got to get groceries soon, baby." She stroked the contented feline from the M-shaped mark on his forehead to the tip of his twitching tail. "You've got plenty, but mama's cupboards are bare." Cecily cradled the bowl of a full wine glass in her palm and stepped out under the skylights of her heated sun porch. The biggest and brightest stars in a clear sky shimmered in defiance of the city's artificial glare. Cecily raised the glass to her lips, glanced over the rim, and jumped at the unexpected movement beyond the window.

"Damn it!" She wiped sloshed wine from her chin and the cowl neck on the beige sweater under it. "Of course, it had to be red." Cecily licked her fingers and unlocked the back door. The knob turned.

"Hey, girlfriend." Kelly walked through and closed the door. "I figured you'd be back here."

Cecily gathered up and moved a pile of papers in file folders from Kelly's preferred egg-shaped chair in the corner. "How did you know I was home?"

"The lights are on. That old Camaro nobody else would own but you is parked across the street, and it's Wednesday night. You never go out on a Wednesday. And you always sit out here."

Cecily grunted. "Am I really that predictable?"

"In a word, yes." Kelly kicked off her ankle boots and settled into quilted comfort. "Didn't get my message? Or did you lose your phone again?"

"I didn't lose it. I only use it to order pizza. Which is on the way, by the way." Cecily licked her fingers and dabbed at the stain on her sweater. "I saw your text. What's so urgent that you couldn't wait for a reply?"

"I need some advice."

"I need more wine. And to properly wipe off what I spilled. Can I get you a glass?"

Kelly shook her head. "Nope. I'm driving. But I will take a ginger ale if you've got it."

"That's about all I do have." Cecily returned from the kitchen with a can of soda and the bottle of wine. "So, what's up? Don't tell me you're getting cold feet about marrying Eddie. Because if you don't, I will."

Kelly laughed. "Not a chance. Besides, you're too old for him."

"I've only got about ten years on him. That's not too old. Haven't you heard? Some men prefer a more mature, worldly, and seasoned woman."

"You're built like Beyonce, and the farthest you've ever been from Chicago was a wedding in Milwaukee."

"Not true. I went to Disney World with the family when I was sixteen." Cecily sat in an identical chair opposite her friend. "Speaking of weddings, have you and Eddie set a date?"

Kelly opened but didn't drink from her can of soda. Her finger traced the aluminum rim. "Not yet."

"Why not?" *I think I know why. The question is, my friend, do you?* "What's the hold up?"

"I gotta work through some things first." Kelly set the can down on the glass-top table between them. "I need to talk to you about something else. A case Eddie and I are working on."

Cecily listened as Kelly relayed a condensed version of a case starved for clues and top-heavy with hearsay. Cecily's eyebrows lifted with concern about what her friend wasn't saying. "So, what you're telling me is you and Eddie have nothing to go on but suspicions. And your client doesn't want to get the police involved. No missing person report because the missing person is most likely in the country illegally."

"That's about it."

"Wow." Cecily looked down and into her empty wine glass. "Do you know anything about the woman your client is looking for? Her name? Approximate age? If, where, and how long she's been in Chicago?"

"Lucas didn't find out much when he was in Buenos Aires. Her last name is Vasquez. The owner of a store in the neighborhood where she grew up referred to her as Rayen. The last time the shopkeeper saw her, she was maybe in her mid-twenties. But apparently, she's been gone for a while."

"Well," Cecily refilled her wine glass, "the good news is human traffickers in the sex trade want them younger than that."

"Do you think that's how she got here?" Kelly asked.

Cecily nodded. "It's a very real possibility. If that's what happened to her, she's most likely a domestic slave worker either kept by a manager or paid enough to live but not enough to leave."

Kelly frowned. "That sounds grim."

"It is that."

"So, how do we find out where she is?"

"If Rayen sent that money order to Argentina, then she has to be within walking distance of that bodega. She wouldn't have enough money for taxi or bus fare, especially if she's been saving what little she gets to send back home."

"The guy behind the counter said they don't send wire transfers from there."

"He was lying. Bodegas like that one will do anything out of a back room for a price. That's where we start."

"We?"

"You didn't traipse past my window just to scare the bejesus out of me. We've got history. I work in courtrooms now, but you know me. Once a detective, always a detective." The conversation paused at the doorbell chime. "That's my pizza. You hungry?"

"I'll take a slice." Kelly wrinkled her nose. "But you can have the anchovies."

"And I'll take 'em." Cecily got up to pay for dinner. "In my book, wasting little salty fish is a crime."

Chapter 9

The Snitch

Octavio Hernandez hated the Hispanic whose seed had spawned him. He spoke Spanish only when doing so would advance his profit and reputation as a kingpin to be feared. He made his mark on the savage streets of Chicago's South Side early, transported from Arizona by a trafficker at age nine. The dirty deeds of his fierce hustle more than compensated for Octavio's squat stature and muscles disguised under folds of fatty bulk. Atypically blonde and blue-eyed, he rejected the past and took the name of his German maternal grandfather. After ruthlessly killing a competitor in the begging ring, no one dared speak his given name again. Octavio had died. Otto Hermann was born.

The crooked left index finger, broken by a punch that had cost a liar an eye, traced the indent and edges of a jagged scar on his cheek. The wound inflicted in a knife fight had healed without stitches. His opponent wasn't so lucky. He'd spit blood and died with the knife between his ribs. Otto leaned back in the chair at his desk, covered his mouth with his hand, and faked a yawn. "I'm a busy man. This interruption had best be worth my time."

"We had visitors at the bodega today." The clerk stuffed a plug of tobacco between his cheeks and gum. "Private dicks. A blanquito and his chava asking questions."

42

The diagonal scar from temple to upper lip stretched with the rise of Otto's pale eyebrow. "About."

"Money wired to Buenos Aires." The bodega clerk rapped chapped knuckles on the smooth surface that separated them. "From a chamaca last name Vasquez."

Otto's cheeks fired red. "Who took the money?" His fist halted an inch away from the tip of the startled messenger's nose. "Who sent it?"

The bodega clerk backed away from the pungent fried onion and garlic smell on his boss' breath. "No lo se. I don't know. It happened weeks ago. In the back. I didn't see it go down."

The desk drawer slid open. The dreaded revolver appeared. "Find out!" The clerk hid wide-eyed fear behind raised hands, palms forward in a show of surrender. "Don't show your face again until you can deliver whoever it was to me." Otto turned his back on the clerk's rapid exit. Hard heels on the soles of his shoes drummed an ominous beat across the scuffed floorboards. "Rayen!" He cursed the echo of emptiness. "Where is that bitch?" He jogged down a flight of stairs to the building's ground level. Three hard kicks and a shoulder slam splintered the frame around the first door on the right.

Rayen dropped the bowl of rice cooked on a hot plate and the opened single-serving carton of milk. It spilled and shattered in a splintered mix of food, liquid, and cheap pottery at her feet. The open-hand slap across her face spun her around and against a concrete block wall in the one room she occupied.

"Where's the rest of it?" Otto ripped the sheet and blanket from the single mattress on a wobbly metal frame. Foam mushroomed from the pillow casing he tore apart. Loose fronts from drawers in the dresser Rayen had rescued from a dumpster came off in Otto's hands. He scooped out and scattered underwear, socks, and a flannel nightgown on the cement floor that Rayen could not scrub clean.

She cowered as he charged, raised her hands in self-defense, and cried out at the pain of his fingers twisted in her hair.

"Where is the rest of it?" He repeated the demand.

"I don't know what you mean." The words caught in her throat, constricted by terror.

"The money you stole from me." He flattened her to the wall with the press of his body.

"I don't steal." Rayen struggled to breathe.

43

He snorted like a raging bull and spat in her face. "Do you expect me to believe you saved and wired the pittance I paid you back to Argentina?"

His hands at her throat lifted and squeezed. The jagged scar from the tip to the bridge of his nose invaded her fading vision. Her arms went limp. His knee between her thighs forced her legs apart.

He will not rape me! she screamed in her head. *I'd rather die!*

She lashed out with the only weapon she had. Her teeth sunk into flesh. She tasted blood. Otto roared, released her, and backed away. The gash in the reopened scar flowed fresh ribbons of stain to the collar of his white shirt. Otto wiped his nose. Blood smeared his sleeve.

"You'll work for nothing until I'm paid back in full!" he screamed. "Try to leave, and I'll kill you." He turned and lurched through the remains of the door.

Rayen slid down the wall, hugged her knees, and sat on the cold floor. She listened and waited until the only sounds came from the city outside. She crawled over the mangled heap of what little she had and curled into a fetal position on the naked mattress. A pool of light from the street, diffused through a rectangle of glass coated by urban grime, shone through nailed-shut windows that would never open to let air in or her out.

Her mind formed a plan of escape in the darkness. Her renewed, desperate promise repeated in a mantra of resolve. "I will find him, mama," she whispered. "We will come back for you."

Chapter 10

Unmistakable M.O.

Detective Jim Ross started this day as he had every day since he'd bought a new set of golf clubs. He crossed off another date on the calendar countdown to retirement from the Chicago PD.

"Long night?" Jim rounded the desk across from his and clapped his partner on the shoulder.

Paul Callaway slumped in his chair over a half-gone third cup of coffee consumed in the first hour of their shift. "You could say that." He rubbed his bloodshot eyes and groaned as he stood and stretched his long legs and arms.

"Sex takes it out of the legs first." Jim laughed at the indignant huff. He stepped toward the briefing room and grinned at the shuffle that replaced the usual spring of Paul's footsteps.

"All hands on deck for the morning briefing." Jim glanced up as Sergeant Brenda Talbot entered the room with a leather-bound notebook tucked under her arm and a stack of paper in her hands. The Navy veteran who'd served her country in Persian Gulf combat zones used the vernacular of her first career when relevant to the station house situation.

His first impression of his new commanding officer was far from politically correct. *Now here's a broad to be reckoned with*; he'd thought when the forty-something woman of color was introduced to the ranks she would command.

Her steely persona stood taller and projected strength greater than her medium height and lean build.

"Good morning." Sergeant Talbot dropped a stack of paper on the table at the front of the room and moved around the six-foot-long barrier to address her urban troops in uniform and plain clothes. She opened her notebook and delivered a clipped review of the previous shift reports and suspects in lockup for crimes ranging from petty theft and public nuisance to armed robbery and assault. "Final note calls attention to activity likely related to people trafficking. The managers in the south want to expand their sex trade and sales crew peddling rings to reach potential clients in more affluent areas. Managers in the north and east to the lake shore aren't rolling out the welcome mats. We need to disarm this advance before it becomes an all-out turf war." The sergeant tapped the pile of paper on her right. "Details are in the report. It's not pretty. Be safe. Work smart. Go home tonight."

Paul got to the pile first. "This kind of shit makes me sick." He handed a copy to Jim.

"From the looks of you, that wouldn't take much." Jim skimmed through enough of what was on the printout to get the message. "Mostly minor disturbances. No solicitation signs ignored by merry bands of aggressive a-holes. Girls painted up to look like women hustling tricks from doorways and street corners." Jim flipped the page over. "No guns. Seems knives are the weapons of choice."

"Yeah, I saw that," Paul said. "Like a West Side Story rumble."

The gruesome discovery of a human hand in a dumpster behind a restaurant serving Argentine cuisine got Jim's attention. "Huh." Ross rubbed his chin.

Paul picked up on his partner's signal. "What are you thinking?" he asked.

"The tips were cut off the fingers on the hand in the dumpster. No prints. Tougher to ID. Reminds me of a case I worked on years ago. Way back in the first year I had my gold shield. Same MO. Severed hand with the ends of the fingers missing from the top knuckle. Took weeks to find the rest of the body and months to put a name to the remains."

Paul followed Jim through the maze of desks and workstations. The partners settled in chairs behind desks placed close enough to avoid the need to shout over periodic unpredictable chaos. "Well, it won't take months to find out who belongs to this hand."

Jim nodded. "True enough. Thank you, DNA forensics."

"So, what else can you tell me about that cut-off fingers case from the dark ages?" Paul asked.

"Ha ha." Jim sat back and squinted his eyes. "As I recall, the dead kid was a drug runner. Small-time stuff. No big drops. Tried to go big and lost. I arrested a real badass with a Latino last name. Hernando or Herreras. Something like that. Had blue eyes and a head of blonde hair." He tapped his computer's keyboard. A quick search of the year rookie Detective Ross would never forget delivered a digital file with a name and face attached. "Yeah, that's him. He was a juvenile at the time. Slippery as hell. The case didn't go to court. He worked the system and was back on the street in eighteen months."

Paul stood over his partner's shoulder and studied the screen. "Where's this badass kid now?"

"Good question." Jim searched Chicago PD's database and came up empty. "Huh. He either reformed or relocated."

"Or hid behind an alias," Paul said.

"Good point." Jim jotted down the name he had and closed the digital file.

Chapter 11

The Stakeout

The blue-gray dome of mid-afternoon winter hung over the rooftops of row houses and storefronts. Vehicles parked inches from front and rear fenders, clogged curbs along the narrow two-way street. Kelly was slumped in the Jeep's passenger side seat and stared at the bodega's front door, a tow-away zone from the Jeep's front bumper. She gritted her teeth and fought the temptation to scream *I hate stakeouts! I hate being back here!*

"You still awake?" Eddie was in the driver's seat beside her. He clicked the shutter and lowered the camera to his lap. He reached over and lightly squeezed her knee.

Kelly shivered.

"Are you cold, babe?"

"Kind of."

"Why didn't you say something?" The shot of warm air through the vent fogged up the car windows.

"That's why." Kelly flipped the system to defrost. The windows cleared. Movement in the side mirror nudged her curiosity. Kelly watched a woman she guessed to be about her age and height cross about a half block away in the middle of the residential street. The long black coat she wore hung on her thin frame. She hugged a cloth bag with wide light blue and white stripes tight against her chest. The woman paced the sidewalk as though trying to decide on a direction. She stepped back into the street, then abruptly turned, hurried to the corner, and ducked under the bodega's red awning. Kelly checked the time on her Fitbit. The woman came back through the bodega's front door three minutes and twenty-seven seconds later. The blue and white bag was gone. "That's weird." Kelly poked Eddie's arm.

"What?"

"Follow that woman in the black coat."

"Why?"

"Just follow her, OK?"

"OK." Eddie dropped the idling Jeep into gear and pulled away from the curb ahead of a slow-moving truck marked U-Haul. "Now, will you tell me why?"

"Why would someone walk into a bodega with a bag, presumably to go shopping, and walk out with nothing? Not even the bag."

"Good question, Watson." Eddie passed the camera to Kelly and cranked the Jeep's steering wheel. Horns honked at the sudden flash of brake lights and right turn. "Let's find out."

Eddie drove a slow, deliberate pattern through moderate traffic. Kelly pointed the camera's lens through the windshield's glass. Steady surveillance tracked the woman's apparent deliberate progression along the inside edge of sidewalks closest to walls, steps, and the occasional front porch. "She's going down that alley. See her?"

"Yeah. Obviously, I can't follow her without being noticed. I'll have to go around the block and hope she comes out the other end." Eddie steered the car around corners and dodged a boy on a bicycle with a wobbly front wheel. In the split second of that diversion, the woman in the black coat ran from the alley and out in front of the Jeep. "Holy shit!" Eddie slammed on the brakes. Kelly snapped the camera's shutter.

Eddie opened the driver's side window. "Hey! Are you OK?" he shouted to the woman. Flattened palms and spread fingers on the car's hood kept her upright and off the pavement. Her dark eyes were wide open, and her pale lips moved with no answer. She turned and ran back down the alley.

The driver of the white panel van behind the Jeep blasted the vehicle's horn and shouted, "Move it, asshole!"

"Fuck off," Eddie grumbled.

Kelly squinted through the camera's zoom lens. "We've lost her."

"Yeah, tell me something I don't know."

"Go back around the block."

Eddie's previous tactic didn't work a second time. No one on the sidewalks within a several-block radius matched her description. Late November shadows of early evening shifted the feel of the South Side streets from unseemly to ominous. Eddie looked for an exit to the north lake shore and home. "I guess there's no point in returning to the bodega."

Kelly blew out a sigh of relief. "Well, the day wasn't a total bust." She brought up the last image captured by the camera. "For whatever it's worth, I got this." The image of a frightened Latina with eyes nearly as black as her blunt cut, chin-length hair was framed in minute digital detail. "I wonder who she is."

"I'm just glad we didn't find out the hard way." Eddie gripped the steering wheel. The residual tremble in his hands from delayed reaction calmed. "If she's in the country legally, we might be able to get an ID through facial recognition. But if she's not, which I strongly suspect is the case, that bit of PI work won't be so easy."

"I'll start in the usual places. If the online search leads nowhere, I'll call Cecily."

"Your forensic psych friend? What can she do?"

"Cecily was a detective before she went to law school and got her PhD. She knows the law, and she knows the streets."

"Was she Chicago PD?"

She felt her chest tighten. "That's what she told me."

"You told me Cecily helped you with your forensics thesis while she was working on her clinical psych dissertation." Eddie signaled for a lane change and glanced at Kelly. "Did you know her when she was a cop?"

Her mind drifts briefly—"I chased down the last lead I had. Nothing. Not a damn thing." Kelly couldn't remember who cried first or for how long. "I am so, so sorry, Kelly. I don't know who killed your brother. But I promise you, I'll never stop looking."

"No." Breath caught in Kelly's throat. Her stomach cramped. Kelly swallowed and told another lie. "I met Cecily after she'd passed the bar exam."

"Jim might know when she got her shield."

"He would since she was his partner," a reveal Kelly immediately regretted.

Eddie's jaw set. His face flushed. "She told you that, too? Why didn't you tell me?"

Every reason Kelly could think of would be another lie. So, she stared straight ahead at the steady stream of tail lights. "Can we please change the subject?"

Eddie frowned and fixed his gaze on the road and traffic ahead. "Fine." The strained silence between them continued through dinner and beyond. He ran off his frustrations pounding the pavement along the pathway bordered by North Lake Shore Drive and Lake Michigan. She buried hers in the rapid tap of fingers on a keyboard. Kelly downloaded the photo and sifted through websites and databases that could put a name to the face in the image.

"Anything?" Eddie stood in the doorway to her home office.

"Nope." She turned in her chair and felt the heat rise in places that only he could touch. Her fiancé. Fresh from a shower after his daily run. Covered only by a towel from his navel to his knees.

"Can't say I'm surprised." He removed the towel and used it to scrub his comb-over mid-length hair dry. Overhead light from the hallway accentuated the dips and curves of lean naked muscle. "Did you call her?"

"Who?" *Wow. The distraction of him had diverted all of her.*

"Cecily."

"Text message with the photo attached." Kelly hit send on her laptop. "Done."

Eddie crossed the room toward Kelly and cinched the towel around his waist.

"Oh, don't do that."

"Don't do what?"

"This." Kelly took the towel away and dropped it to the floor. What she wore topped the pile.

Chapter 12

Puzzle Pieces

The sharp shift in wind direction off Lake Michigan caught and opened the unzipped front of Jim's flannel-lined windbreaker. Cold rain pelted his shirt.

"Dammit!" Jim zipped up the jacket and lifted the yellow crime scene tape. Rotating lights mounted on bars on top of squad cars flashed eerie blue and red patterns on spiked grass framed by hard city surface. Harsh white beams from spotlights exposed newly-trenched earth. Forensics personnel in hazmat suits crawled in and scraped the open crevice.

"What have we got?" Jim stood beside Sergeant Bill Collier, commanding officer from a neighboring district station house. The veteran cops had come up the ranks together. Each had earned respect acknowledged by commendations. Both were counting down the days to full pension.

Bill flipped the collar on his raincoat and shoved his hands in his pockets. "Utility crew installing fiber optic dug up body parts on both sides of our lines."

"I guess that means we're both working this case," Jim said.

"You guessed right."

Bags tagged for transport to the morgue passed from investigators in the muddy unmarked grave to the gloved hands of police officers. "One victim?"

"Won't know until the site is clear and the medical examiner puts all the recovered pieces together."

"Hey, Sarge." A young officer Jim didn't recognize called to his CO from the mud mound surrounding a fresh dig. "I think you should have a look at this."

Jim and Bill dodged wide cracks and potholes filled and disguised by dark water. Workers leaned on shovels used to reclaim remains. The officer pointed at what had been revealed in the shallow pit. Two heads severed from the victims' bodies. Both were blown open by a gun fired at close range.

"There's your answer, Ross."

Jim scratched his balding head and swiped the dampness from the hair he still had. "Another case, a bigger question."

"How do you mean?" Bill asked.

"I mean, it could be this case is connected to the severed hand in the restaurant's dumpster with the fingertips cut off."

"That could be another missing piece. No casings recovered, or witness reports of gunfire at that scene. But there wouldn't be if the murder happened somewhere else." Bill nodded at the carnage. "You think maybe the rest of the body is here?"

"If there's one thing I've learned in thirty-odd years on the force, anything is possible." Sudden heavy rain pounded the ground like bullets from a lead-filled sky. Jim and Bill ran for the cover of Jim's unmarked sedan. Warm breath and humidity rising from their soaked clothes condensed to form rivulet trails on the interior of the rolled-up windows.

"We done here?" Jim asked.

Bill brushed the rain from the folds of his coat. "I sure as hell am."

"I'll drop you off at your house and head back to mine." Jim navigated the semi-flooded streets of the North Side, windshield wipers on full speed slap.

Bill swiped at the passenger's side window with his coat sleeve. "Talk to me. What's your take on this?"

Jim swerved to avoid a dancing manhole cover lifted by the pressure of rushing rainwater. "All I've got is a bad feeling and a hunch. Remember a blonde juvie with a Latino name I collared right after we got our shields?"

"Yeah. Ugly mug. Killed a kid and walked. What about him?"

"He still around?"

Bill grunted. "Disappeared after Homeland Security put out a BOLO on him and three other gang bangers for trafficking cocaine across state lines and borders."

"When was this?"

"I don't know. Five. Maybe six years ago."

"That's a long time to fly under the radar anywhere."

"What are you suggesting?"

Jim pulled to the curb in front of the station house Bill commanded. "Maybe that piss ant from my past is tied up in this missing parts body count."

"How did you make that connection?"

"Think about it. A hand with no body attached or anywhere nearby. That's a gang trademark. A maim or kill warning. Don't fuck with the boss. It fits that mutt's previous MO. What bothers me is the dismemberment, and execution-style evidence planted just over the line with ours. And out of what was his. Tells me that if he's still around, he's not satisfied with staying on his turf. Or cutting up his victims."

"Now he's got guns." Bill sighed and shook his head. "You're probably right." He opened the car door. "But damn, I hope you're wrong."

***

Paul looked up from the pile of paperwork on his desk and snickered at his partner's damp and disheveled state. "Go through a car wash with the windows down?"

"No, smartass, I took a shower with my clothes on to save time." Jim peeled off the wet windbreaker and plopped into the chair behind his desk.

Paul laughed. "That's a good one. So, was it worth getting soaked to the bone?"

"Yes and no. The evidence is with the ME." Jim frowned at the post-it note stuck in the congealed dregs at the bottom of his coffee cup. "Dumpster DNA." Jim picked up the cup. "Ha. Ha. Very funny."

"I just call 'em like I see 'em."

Jim grumbled and picked the note out of the sludge. "You got anything?"

Paul nodded. "The DNA report on Thing is on your desk."

"Thing?"

"You know. The hand that came out of the box and delivered the mail on *The Addams Family*. Becca and I binge watched every episode of that show last weekend."

"Becca." Jim's eyebrows rose with the corners of his mouth. "Finally—a name attached to the reason for your heavy legs."

"Yeah, well, whatever." Paul swiveled in his seat. The metallic squawk from the chair's hardware sounded like mock laughter. "It's nothing serious."

"Hey, all work and no sex ain't living." Jim tossed the post-it note in the trash. "I should know," he muttered and scanned the report's contents. "Huh." Jim rubbed the stubble on his chin. "Carlos Delgado. Not one of Chicago's most upstanding citizens. But that mutt didn't deserve this."

"No one does. You know him?"

"Informant way back in the day." He leaned back in the chair and slapped the file folder on the desk. "Weasel with a laundry list of petty crime convictions. Enough cash, and he'd squeal on anybody. Wonder who he sold out this last time." Jim lifted the receiver on his desk phone and called Sergeant Collier. "Yeah, Bill. It's Jim. Got another piece to the puzzle. Was Carlos Delgado working with anybody in your house?"

His friend hesitated, said he wasn't sure, promised to call back, and hung up. "Huh." Jim stared at the receiver and wondered what devil was in the detail he didn't know yet.

Chapter 13

The Delivery

Unfamiliar streets frightened the boy. So did words shouted and spoken in phrases and questions he did not understand. He picked at the grime under his fingernails and stared at the cigarette butts, crushed cups, and balls of ketchup and mustard-stained wrappers littering the bus stop shelter. Remnants of a nicotine habit that made his eyes water and his nose itch. Trash with printed words he could not read.

He got off the bench at the grind of brakes and the hiss of the bus door opening. He climbed metal stairs with the yellow strip ground down by the soles of shoes and handed the bus driver the token she'd given him the day before. Squeezed into an aisle seat four rows from the back on the left, his thin arms ached from hugging the cloth bag and what was in it so tightly to his chest. He'd promised her he wouldn't let go. Not if his life depended on it.

He counted the stops as she'd instructed. This many more to the building he'd never entered on a street where he'd never been. He flowed with the funneled crush of commuters out of the bus and into the Windy City's primary business artery and walked into the sixty-four-story structure that scraped the blue-sky dome over the Loop. He waited for the elevator doors to open.

"What floor?" The older lady in the black and white plaid coat wore gloves as grey as the tightly wound curls that poked out from under the brim of her black felt hat. She smelled like lilacs and raindrops. He didn't know the words to say. Only the numbers.

"Two. Four. Zero. Zero."

"Two four zero zero." Thin lips nearly disappeared in her confusion. "Suite 2400?" she asked.

Panic rippled through him. His chin dipped toward his chest. *Did she understand his nod meant yes?*

He faced the closing doors. Felt the elevator lift. Heard the soft whish and ping as the doors parted. Glad to be on solid ground again, he scanned the hallway for a door with the numbers. Two. Four. Zero. Zero. Cool metal resisted his push. He pressed his hands on the clean glass.

"Can I help you?" The woman behind the big desk was young and pretty. He liked the red and white lapel pin on her suit jacket and the flag with a red maple leaf at its center.

He held out the bag with blue and white stripes and a golden sun. "Lucas Dominguez." The boy winced at the adolescent crackle in his voice that he could no longer control.

The pretty woman's smile turned down. "I'm sorry. He's not here at the moment."

The boy stood as straight and tall as the tremble in his legs would allow. "Lucas Dominguez," he repeated.

"Just a moment." She got up and stepped past the desk to an open office door. Her legs were long. Her skirt wasn't. He tried not to stare.

"Craig, can you come out here, please?" A middle-aged man in a blue suit and matching tie over buttons on a white shirt followed her. "I think the bag this young man has is for Lucas."

"Si! Si!" *They understood!* "Para Lucas Dominguez de Sherbrooke Quebec Canada." He'd recited the words they'd rehearsed together until he got it exactly right. The man in the blue suit took the bag.

Done! The worn heels of his sneakers squeaked with his pivot.

"Wait!" the man in the suit called out.

He didn't. The doors marked Consulate General of Canada opened with his shoulder shove. He rode the elevator to the lobby, fisted the bus token in his pocket, and ran toward the stop that would return him to where what and who he knew.

Chapter 14

The Mate Cup

Green eyes with black pupil slits stared over the edge of the wood table horizon.

Cecily tried to ignore him. "You know, this would be seriously annoying behavior if you weren't so damn adorable."

Cornelius didn't blink.

"OK, I get the message." Cecily lowered the lid on her laptop and padded across the floor in thick wool socks behind her companion's silent paws and vertical tail twitch. He licked his lips and whiskers as the scoop of kibble filled the bowl.

"Lunchtime is as good as any for a sandwich." Cecily twisted the tie on the wrapper, opened the plastic covering the loaf of bread, and groaned. "Green again." She closed the bag and tossed what would have been her midday meal into the garbage. "This is why I don't buy groceries, kid," she told her cat. "I throw out more than I eat." Cecily sniffed the jug of milk from the fridge. Satisfied the contents were drinkable, she poured a full glass and returned to the tedium of reviewing court cases and police reports and the task of matching facts with a face.

"Once more with feeling." Cecily logged in and scrolled through pages of information from Cook County, Illinois, on persons of interest in illegal immigration and human trafficking. The face that paused her finger on the mouse didn't belong to Rayen. Cecily clicked on an image attached to a Department of Homeland Security report and read the caption.

These individuals associated with gang activity in the city of Chicago clearly pose a significant threat to public safety. Ramon Gutierrez. Hector Arroyo. Octavio Hernandez.

"This blonde-haired fucker looks familiar." She read the caption out loud. "Octavio Hernandez. Now, where have I seen that face before?" The cell phone next to her laptop lit up. Kelly's name flashed on the caller ID display. "Hey, friend. What's up?"

"I'm asking you. Did you find out who she is?"

"I'm working on it." Cecily closed the laptop. "I'm bored out of my mind and about half blind from trying."

"Well, stop what you're doing and drive up to Lake Bluff."

"When?"

"Uh, now. Our clients Lucas and Tori are on their way to our office. He's got something he wants to show us. Eddie and I will make the trip north worth your while. Dinner's on us."

Cecily's stomach gurgled. "Since lunch was a glass of milk, how can I refuse? I'll see you soon." She considered and dismissed a change of clothes from casual stay-at-home, grabbed the parka from the closet, and stuffed her feet into boots kicked off earlier at the door. She covered close-cropped wiry curls with a stocking cap and slung purse straps over her shoulder. On second thought impulse, Cecily tucked the laptop under her arm. "You're on your own, buddy boy," she called out to Cornelius. "Don't do anything I would." The security system clicked on as the locked front door closed.

A missed exit and detour delayed Cecily's arrival at The UnMatchables agency. The meeting in progress resumed with introductions and an apology accepted.

Cecily settled in the leather chair identical to the one next to hers that Kelly occupied. Lucas and Tori huddled on the sofa across from them, his fingers laced with hers. Eddie wheeled his desk chair to sit beside Kelly. The low table in the center of the meeting space displayed an empty cloth bag dyed with colors and a symbol Cecily recognized and a flat-bottomed, round-in-the-middle, hollowed-out gourd. A silver straw protruded from the lip of the thumb-sized metal ring on top. "Interesting mate cup," Cecily said. "It looks well used. May I?"

Lucas nodded. "Of course." The sadness in his eyes overshadowed his smile. "It belonged to the Ruiz family. They were my family's neighbors and friends."

The feather-light cup in Cecily's hand fit in her palm. Vibrant colors and symbols painted on the brown gourd represented the landscape, wildlife, and Argentine culture of respect and tradition of sharing. The green leaves of the dried yerba plant steeped for tea. The mountains, birds, and beasts fed by Pampas grass. The joined hands and scales of justice that had not always served the people well. "It's lovely. Reminds me of one my Nana got from a foreign exchange student she hosted." She handed the cup back to Lucas. "Nana treasured that gift."

Lucas took the cup from Cecily and held it as he would a relic that could shatter at the slightest touch. "I remember this cup passed at family dinners and celebrations or sometimes for no reason at all. Camila Ruiz saved it from the destruction of our homes and our country by the military. She brought it with her to Canada, then took it back to Argentina." Lucas returned the cup to its resting place on the cloth bag. "The cup and this bag were delivered by a young boy to the Chicago office of the Consulate of Canada two days ago. I regret that I was not there at the time."

"How did this boy get the cup?" Cecily asked.

"Camila's daughter Adriana returned to Buenos Aires with her mother. I have reason to believe either Adriana or her daughter Rayen gave it to him to deliver to me. It's the only possible explanation."

Cecily nodded in agreement. "Did this messenger ask for you by name?"

"Yes. He spoke Spanish. He said the package was for Lucas Dominguez of Sherbrooke, Quebec. That's where what was left of my family and the Ruiz family settled when we immigrated to Canada."

"So, I take it he didn't know you were working at the consulate."

"I don't believe so, no. It's not public knowledge. My government keeps that information confidential."

"Well, this puts a new spin of urgency on the investigation." Cecily set her laptop on the table. "Have you shown him the photo?"

Eddie shifted in the chair and cleared his throat. "Not yet. We were leading up to that."

"What photo?" Lucas asked.

Cecily opened the laptop, tapped the keyboard, and brought up the image. "This photo." She turned the monitor around for Lucas to see.

"Adriana!" The invisible two-fisted sucker punch of recognition and disbelief overwhelmed him. "It can't be her. I know it can't be her." Powerful waves of visceral emotion threatened to drown him.

"Lucas!" Tori held on to him.

"I'm alright, mon amour." Slowly he recovered and took her hands in his. Inhaled deeply and let a breath out slowly. He studied the photo. "This must be Rayen." He looked from Eddie to Kelly. "Where was this taken?"

Eddie leaned forward, elbows on his knees. "A few blocks away from the bodega where the money order was wired from."

"Then Rayen must have sent it," Lucas said.

"You just confirmed our working theory," Kelly responded.

Cecily drummed the tips of long polished nails on the arms of the chair. "Let's talk this out. Gather the pieces and put together what we've got so far. If Rayen had the mate cup and she doesn't know Lucas is in Chicago, then we have a real-time crunch problem to contend with."

"How so?" Eddie asked.

"Having the cup delivered to the consulate is an act of desperation. Rayen is probably in the country illegally without a passport or any other form of ID. When she left Argentina, her likely destination was Canada. The only contact name she had was yours, Lucas. She was on her way to you and only got this far. I've seen my fair share of cases like this working with the district attorney's office. Here's my theory. She's a victim of human trafficking recruited into domestic slavery with the promise of work for the cash she needed to keep going. Something has happened. Her situation is changing or has changed. She feels threatened. She's scared. Her life may be in danger. She needs to get away, and she's getting ready to run. She sees the Canadian consulate as the only way to get a message to you to let you know that she's on her way again. Whatever her reason, no matter the cost, she's determined to find you."

"So, what you're saying is we've got to get to her before she leaves the city," Kelly said.

"That's right," Cecily said.

"Santa Maria, Madre de Dios," Lucas moaned out the words and pressed his palms together in prayer. "I went to Buenos Aires to bring Adriana and her family back to Quebec. I was too late to help her mother. I don't know yet where Adriana is." He pointed to the image on the laptop screen. "But I know in my heart that she is her daughter. Rayen is here. I can get her to safety. Please," he pleaded, "tell me what I can do."

Eddie glanced from Kelly to Cecily for advice or suggestions. Hearing none, he composed his own. "Lucas, I hear you. God knows if I were in your shoes, I wouldn't be able to sit still and wait. But that's what I'm asking you to do. Give us time to devise a plan and a solid strategy to find her. At least now we know who Rayen is, where she is, and what she looks like. So, we have more to go on than we did an hour ago. I know it's not easy. But you've got to trust us to do everything we can for you and her."

"Lucas," Tori's arm circled his broad, slumped shoulders, "you've done all you can for now. We need to go and let them do what they can."

"Of course, you're right, mon amour." He smiled and lightly kissed her forehead. "You look after me."

"Je t'aime, Lucas."

"Je t'aime aussi, Victoria."

The couple left The UnMatchables office with their arms around each other. Tori cradled the bag with the mate cup packed safely inside.

"We're definitely on the right track," Kelly said. "That bag the cup is in?"

"With the national flag of Argentina on it," Cecily said.

"Is that what that is? Well, I'm ninety-nine percent sure that's the same bag Rayen went into the bodega with fifteen minutes before Eddie almost ran her over."

Eddie frowned. "I beg to clarify. She ran out in front of the car."

Cecily closed her laptop. "Well, my friends, we have got our work cut out for us. I suggest we get started around a table somewhere with menus, wait staff, and generous portions of I really don't care what."

Chapter 15

An Unexpected Intrusion

The air inside Tori's car chilled by degrees with the click of the cooling engine. "I don't think you should be alone tonight, love."

"Then stay with me." The gentle caress of his fingertips traced bare skin from the 'v' in her sweater to the sensitive spot behind her ear. She sighed at the rush of sudden overstimulation.

"Lucas," she breathed at the soft press of his lips where his fingers had been. "I've got to take care of Cassie. Come home with me."

"Here now, there later."

She moaned as his hand and thumb brushed other sensitive points under her coat. "If I go up to your apartment, we won't leave, and I'll have a mess to clean up in the morning."

Breaking glass, a blaring car horn, and the raw cry of rubber grinding cement in accelerated escape abruptly ended their moment.

"What the hell!" Lucas shielded Tori with his body. Cloud cover and darkness sliced by an intermittent moon and lamppost light masked whatever threat remained. The loud, repetitive warning from the violated vehicle covered any sounds made by remaining predators.

"Stay in the car." Lucas opened the passenger's side door. "Lock the doors after me."

"Lucas! Don't go out there!" Tori's plea returned to her with the door slam. "I'm calling the police!" She reached behind the driver's seat and wrestled the cell phone out of her purse. The car horn died during the 9-1-1 call for help.

Movement past the windshield startled her. Recognition relieved her. She punched and released the door locks. Lucas was beside her again. But his fists were clenched as tight as his jaw.

"It was my car, the consulate's car. The windshield is shattered."

Tori tried to take his hand. It wouldn't open. "We should sit tight until the police get here."

"You stay. I'm going to check the apartment."

"Then I'm going with you." Tori took the keys from the ignition and grabbed her purse. She trotted alongside Lucas to keep pace with his long strides on the walkway toward the multiplex building. The disabled security keypad at the entrance was frozen in a green error code. The glass doors opened without a click.

"What's happening?" Knuckles swollen by early-stage arthritis bent around the edge of the door to apartment 105. An elderly woman in a fuzzy pink robe and matching hairnet over bobby-pinned silver curls peaked around the opening. "I thought I heard glass breaking."

"You did, Senora Ruby," Lucas said to her. "My car was vandalized."

"Oh, dear!" Ruby clutched and bunched the robe's collar under her chin. "Maybe one of those men did it."

"What men?" Tori asked her.

"The men I saw through my peephole. I've never seen them before. Are the front doors unlocked? Did they break in?"

"Well ..."

"The police are on the way." Lucas interrupted Tori. "Go back inside, Senora. Everything will be fine."

"Well, if you say so. I'm too nervous. I can't go back to bed. Maybe I'll make a cup of tea." The re-activated security signal on Ruby's closed door turned red.

"There's no point in worrying her," Lucas said. Tori followed him up the stairs and down the hallway. A tall man stood at the apartment door. His jeans hung loose at his hips. The shirt tails and plaid pattern of his wrinkled shirt didn't match. He stared at the door. "One of the tenants called me. Said they heard noises in your apartment. The door was open when I got here," he said to Lucas. "I probably shouldn't have closed it."

Block letters the color of dried blood defaced the surface beneath the brass number 252. Lucas swore an oath in the language he'd learned as a child.

"Lucas?" Tori couldn't read the words. "What does it say? What does it mean?" When Lucas didn't answer, Tori texted Kelly, who got the message as the waiter set plates of appetizers and a specialty pizza on their table. It read. Urgent! Call me ASAP!

"Tori's back to this again," Eddie grumbled.

Cecily slid a slice onto her plate. "I didn't peg Tori as a habitual text offender."

"She wasn't really," Kelly said. "She was just worried about Lucas." Kelly hit redial. The call went to voicemail. "Hey, Tori, it's Kelly. Give me a shout back when you can." Kelly ate a fried pickle chip and wiped her fingers on a napkin. "That's odd. If it's so urgent, why didn't she pick up?"

The cell phone rang seconds later. "Tori, what's up?"

"Oh, Kelly, we just got here. We've called the police!"

"Got where? What's happened?"

"We're at Lucas's apartment. The windshield on his car has been smashed. There's some writing on his apartment door. I can't read it. I think Lucas knows what it means. But he won't tell me!"

"Don't go in the apartment until the police arrive," Kelly told her. "We're still in Lake Bluff. We'll be there as soon as we can." Kelly scooted her chair from the table, stood, and put on her coat. She grabbed her purse and a slice of pizza. "We've gotta run."

"Where?" Eddie signaled the waiter. Kelly was already on her way to the door. "What the hell is going on?" he called after her.

"Whatever it is, it can't be good." Cecily wrapped stacked slices of pizza in a handful of napkins and followed her friends to the parking lot.

Chapter 16

A Warning

Squad cars blocked the entrances to the apartment complex parking. The officer guarding the driveway stepped in front of the Jeep and around the bumper to the driver's side window. "Do you live here?" he asked.

"No," Eddie said, "but we ..."

"Residents only."

Tori trotted toward the Jeep through the crime scene carnival of flashing lights and passing uniforms. "It's OK! They're our friends. I called them. Please," she pleaded with the officer.

"The car behind us, too," Eddie said.

The officer's jaw squared above the blue-collar and black vest. "Pull around. Don't get out."

"Let them pass." Lucas stood beside Tori. He pointed at the identifying rear license plate on his violated vehicle and held up his gold-stamped diplomatic passport. The officer glanced from the plate to the passport and waved Eddie in.

"Much obliged." Eddie acknowledged both his client and the officer and led the way to side-by-side empty slots between lines.

Tori hugged Kelly seconds after she'd closed her car door. "I'm so glad you're here." She nodded at Lucas walking with a uniformed officer toward the building. "We both are."

Eddie inspected the shattered windshield. "Was the car like this when you got here?"

Tori shook her head. "We were sitting in my car when we heard the glass break. Whoever did it got away in a van, I think. I'm not sure. It was too dark and happened so fast."

"Usually does." Cecily checked the rear of the car for damage. She motioned to a young female officer standing a few feet away. "The trunk lock has been punched in. Get forensics over here to dust for prints."

The officer glared at her from under the black bill and checkerboard band on her department-issued hat. "And you are?"

"The best goddamn detective Chicago PD ever lost to a courtroom."

Cecily turned and responded to the familiar voice behind a perpetual scowl. "Hello, you old goat. I see you still have that gold shield. Last I heard, you were counting down the days to turn it in."

Jim Ross grunted at the cadet he'd trained and mentored to a well-deserved gold shield of her own. "Don't have enough saved for that lifetime membership at Pebble Beach."

Cecily laughed. "Let me know when you do. I'll join you for drinks in the clubhouse after a lap swim in the heated pool."

Jim's thumb went up. "Two tall vodka tonics with a twist of lime."

She nodded and winked. "Got that right."

"I've got a reason to be here. What's yours?" Jim asked.

"I'm with them." Cecily tipped an ear toward her shoulder.

Jim looked behind her and groaned. "Oh, you gotta be kidding me." He stepped past her and the car surrounded by forensic unit investigators. "Eddie, what the hell are you doing here?"

"Glad to see you too, buddy." Eddie swiped at the misty drizzle coating his cheeks. "And on such a fine evening." His arm circled Kelly's waist. "Let's get in."

"Whoa." Jim moved to intercept Eddie. "Where do you think you're going?"

"In there," he motioned towards the apartments, "with her. Allow me to introduce our client, Tori Deane. Tori, Detective Jim Ross."

"Pleased to meet you." Tori flipped the hood on her jacket over her dripping hair and damp forehead. "That's my boyfriend's car." She chewed on her lip. "Sounds funny to call Lucas my boyfriend."

"We're going in the building to meet up with our other client," Kelly said.

Jim snapped his fingers. "Oh, now it's coming together. That would be the formerly missing Canadian diplomat whose car has now been trashed and apartment broken into."

"That would be correct," Eddie replied.

"Perfect." Jim bent in a mock bow and held his palm up and fingers extended. "Far be it for me to impede your investigation. Please, after you. But don't get in the way." He grumbled at Cecily's low mocking laughter. "There'll be Mounties at the station house in those bulging britches and ugly hats before I can get my first cup of morning coffee."

They passed more uniforms from the front door to the building's second-level hallway. Lucas was leaning with his back against the wall outside the open door to his apartment. Chin to his chest. Fists clenched. A uniformed officer followed the last of the investigators out. He spoke to Lucas in Spanish. Lucas nodded. Tori went to him. He reached for her and held on.

"Stay here," Jim said to Eddie and Kelly and followed the officer to the stairwell. He didn't object when Cecily tagged along. "So, what have we got?" he asked the officer.

"Looks like only his laptop was taken."

"But that's a big deal, right?" Cecily asked.

"It is when the laptop belongs to the Canadian government."

"Oh, shit," Jim muttered. "I knew it. The house will be crawling with RCMP."

"That's not the worst of it."

"You've got more good news, Officer," Jim read the name tag on his uniform, "Perez?"

"I was born here. My parents came to Chicago fresh off the boat from Cuba. I don't know much South American Latino slang. But I doubt what's on that apartment door is a friendly greeting."

"Any idea what it says?"

He nodded toward Lucas. "He's an Argentine national. Ask him."

"I'll do that. Thanks." Jim rechecked the scene cleared of evidence and secured by department personnel, spoke with Tori then walked with her into the apartment.

Eddie reassured Lucas of Jim's credibility and discretion as a cop and a friend. "Look, Lucas." He motioned to his client and walked alongside Kelly a few steps down the hallway. "I know you didn't want the police involved," he said, "but this has gone way beyond hiring us to find Rayen. Apparently, we've found her. But now it looks like whoever is threatening her has found you."

Lucas rubbed at the deep lines on his forehead. "So it would seem."

Tori emerged carrying a zippered suit bag. "Merci, mon amour," Lucas said, taking the bag from her. "Officer Perez advised that I not stay here tonight," he explained.

"Will you be OK at Tori's place?" Kelly asked.

"I had to call the consulate to inform security of the … theft." Lucas hesitated on the last word. "We will be fine." He lowered his voice. "Please do not say anything to the police about Rayen."

"If her name does come up, it won't come from us," Eddie said. "Client confidentiality. Remember?"

"Of course." Lucas glanced at the door Jim closed behind him. "Is there anything else you need from me, Detective?"

"One more thing." Jim underscored the writing on the door with his finger. "Tell me what this means."

Lucas's jaw tightened. "It's an expression and slang used in Argentina. Roughly translated, la sacaste barata means you got off easy. Boludo is a common term with many meanings. In this context, it is intended as an insult."

"Huh." Jim rubbed the stubble on his chin. "You're sure there's nothing else missing? Just the laptop?"

"Only that."

"Any idea why or who might want it?"

"No." The hard edge in his voice and sudden stern stare confirmed Jim's suspicions that Lucas hadn't told the whole truth.

"OK. Well, then we're done here." Jim watched Lucas and Tori walk toward the stairway through the hallway devoid of shadows. Corners and doorways were bright with strategically placed lighting. Multiple security cameras covered nearly every angle. "Huh," he mumbled again. He noticed Cecily doing the same. "I see you're seeing what I'm seeing."

"There has to be video with some incriminating evidence on it," she said.

"My thoughts exactly," Jim agreed. "I wanna have a talk with that building super if he's still around."

"Let's go find him," Cecily said.

"Me. Not you," Jim said to her. "You turned in your shield."

"Then we'll go with you," Kelly said.

"No, you're not," Jim said. "Take her home, Eddie."

Eddie's blue eyes flashed a darker shade of pissed off. "Lucas and Tori are our clients."

"This is my case." Jim stared his friend down. "As I recall, you were hired by her to find him. So why are The UnMatchables still running up the tab on their billable hours meter?"

"You know I can't tell you that," Eddie replied.

Jim puffed a breath from his cheeks through his lips. "Spare me the lame client confidentiality clause excuse." He followed the three of them to the building's front door. "Have a nice night." Misty fog muted their complaints and the sound of slammed car doors. Satisfied they'd taken his non-negotiable advice, Jim searched for the maintenance man in the plaid shirt. He cornered his prey outside the main floor janitor's closet.

A retractable thin wire cable and thicker ring heavy with keycards and keys with teeth dangled from his belt. "I thought you all were gone."

"I will be." Jim led the keeper of the keys through the lobby and halfway down a main artery hallway. The detective pointed at the security cameras nestled in overhead corners. "I need to see the video from these cameras and the second-floor hallway."

"Not possible." Metal keys jangled. A door opened. Most of the monitors on racks along the wall on the other side of the door were dark. "The software crashed. The upgrade is on back order."

Jim stared at the functioning screens. "So you're telling me only the main exits have working cameras. Not the hallways?"

"That's right. Been that way for a week or so now."

"Great." Jim grumbled. "Just great." He glanced up and pointed at the monitor that displayed the building's front door and damaged keypad. "Get me the video from that camera."

"I'll have to clear it with the owner."

"You do that." Jim pulled an official Chicago PD business card from his topcoat pocket and slapped it in the handyman's hand. "Tell your boss I want it tomorrow, or I'll return with a warrant."

Chapter 17

Brisk Response

Jim swatted the morning alarm to snooze and scooped his cell phone from the bedside table. He tapped the device to life.

"Callaway," the alert voice at the other end of the call answered.

"Christ, man, why so damn formal? Who the hell else would be calling you at this hour?"

"Top of the morning to you, too, detective. Do we gotta roll?"

"No, just a heads-up. Hope that rare mid-week day off was worth it."

"It was. Becca's all moved in."

Jim's eyes fully opened. "Well, that woke me up." He flicked the alarm clock off. "So, you got serious, huh? You lucky bastard."

Paul chuckled. "Thanks. I guess. So, why the need for the heads-up?"

Jim brought his partner up to speed on the case and file they'd likely get. "I can't say exactly why. But I've got a feeling this case is connected to the hand in the dumpster and the body parts buried in the trenches."

"Latino gang war?"

"Some kind of turf battle. And Eddie and Kelly's client from the Canadian Consulate figures into it somehow."

"If that's so, he's pissed in somebody's cornflakes. It's a sure bet the investigation won't stay within our jurisdiction."

71

"You got that right."

Jim's phone blipped. "Incoming, I'd best take it."

"I'm up." Paul hung up.

"Yeah, I bet you are," Jim muttered. He answered the call. "Ross."

"Detective." Sergeant Talbott skipped past good morning. "The RCMP and CSIS are extremely interested in a vehicular vandalism and breaking and entering report with your name on it."

Mounties and Canuck security intelligence? Holy fuck. "On my way."

Chapter 18

Another Early Morning Call

The buzz of Kelly's cell phone across the opposite side of the California king bed woke Eddie. His arm flopped on empty sheets. "Kelly?" Eddie rolled and clawed his way to stop the buzz. "Hello?" he answered without opening his eyes.

"Eddie? Is that you? Hi, it's Tori. I'm sorry. Did I wake you?"

"Yeah. You kinda did. What's up?"

"In all the confusion last night, I forgot to tell you and Kelly about Ruby. She lives in the first-floor apartment off the main entrance to Lucas's building."

"Yeah, we've met her."

"You have? When?"

His eyes opened to darkness untouched by daylight. *Oh, shit! I can't tell her that!* "Uh, well, maybe I'm thinking of someone else."

"That's understandable. You probably meet a lot of people in your line of work."

Good save! She bought it! "What about Ruby?"

"She stopped us before we went up to the apartment last night. She said there were men she hadn't seen before fooling around with the front door security lock. I don't know if the police have talked to her yet. I thought maybe

73

you could? She seemed scared. Lucas tried to calm her down. He didn't want to upset her more."

"OK. Yeah. Good to know. Thanks. I'll tell Kelly. We'll go see Ruby today."

"She may know something to help the police catch whoever did this."

"If she does, I'll have to mention it to Jim."

"You'll let us know, too?"

"Sure will."

"Thanks so much, Eddie. I don't know what we would have done without you and Kelly. Cecily was a big help, too."

"Take it easy, Tori. Give our best to Lucas." Eddie glanced at the phone and groaned at the early hour on its digital readout. "Damn, that woman is an early riser." He tossed back the covers, rubbed away the chill from his arms, and grabbed his robe from the chair where he'd tossed it. A quick barefoot pace down the plush textured hallway carpet found Kelly in her home office, huddled over the keyboard, and staring intently at the monitor. Her lips moved with each keystroke.

"Hey, babe." He stood over her shoulder and squinted at the screen. "What are you doing?"

"Trying to find Lucas's laptop."

"You can do that?"

"It's a government-issued laptop, so, yeah, I can lo-jack it and locate it if I get lucky."

"May I remind you his laptop is not our government's issue. And his government is most likely following the same course of action."

"I know that. I didn't say it would be easy." She rolled her shoulders and flexed her wrists.

"I got pretty good at uncovering secrets and buried treasure doing corporate HR background checks for ten soul-sucking years. Given enough time, I can get to this particular hunk of gold before they will. No problem."

He massaged the nape of her neck with the tips of his fingers. "How long have you been at this?"

"I don't know. An hour. Maybe two." She groaned at the pressure of his hands kneading her knotted neck muscles. "I need coffee."

He kissed where his hands had been. "You need to come back to bed with me."

"I'm not tired."

"Who says we'll go back to sleep?" He tugged at the loose knot silk sash that held her robe together. Soft hands cupped her breasts covered by thin cotton. His thumbs circled her nipples. He felt her sigh and went down for more. He knew she wore nothing under the nightgown with the hem that barely stopped at the top of her thighs. Kelly preferred to sleep mostly uncovered.

The pulse under his lips and tongue at her neck quickened and throbbed in rhythm with what his fingers between her legs caressed. She leaned back, and his lips closed over hers. Kelly clutched his hand and led him to their bed. She toppled him to the down duvet-covered mattress and opened his robe. Her thick, untamed mane of honey-blonde hair blanketed her shoulders. Hazel eyes shone a wicked mix of brownish grey and muted green.

"You first." She teased him from a high kneel straddle, her knees on the bed below his waist. Her fingertips played him like an Irish penny whistle. The sensual music stopped at brief intervals with her hands on either side of his head and her breast at his lips. He arched his back and groaned. Downward pressure from his hands on her hips sought relief and release.

"Is this what you want?" She lowered herself and took all of him in stillness. He quivered within her, moved with her as she rode him, easy to urgent. He cried out her name and breathed to recovery while she lay on his chest.

"Kelly, the love of my life, the best friend and partner I've ever had, in business and bed."

"Yes, Eddie, back at you. I'll love you forever."

"When are you going to marry me?"

She rolled to her back and stared at the ceiling. "Can we please not talk about this now?"

"When are we going to talk about it?" Eddie reached for and held her hand tight, anticipating resistance. "Can we at least pick a month? A season? A year?"

"I've got a few things to work through first."

"What things?" He eased over and propped up on his elbow. "Are you afraid I'll relapse? I haven't had a drink in years."

"I know, and I'm proud of you for that."

"If it's the Emerson family money, I've told you. I'm willing to give that up in a heartbeat. We'll move out of the penthouse. Get a place my father doesn't own. To hell with the uber-security and all the bells and whistles."

"That security saved our lives. Besides," she gently tugged on his earlobe, "I rather like the bells and whistles."

"Then what is it? What's keeping us from setting a date?"

Caleb's laugh rang silent. Her father's face blurred invisible. *They weren't there to witness my first two mistakes. It didn't matter because I knew it wasn't love. I knew it wouldn't last. But this time, it's real. I want them to be real! There with me. With us! I need them to be happy for us!* "Just give me a little more time. Please, Eddie."

The crease across his forehead relaxed. But the worry lines between his eyes remained. He forced the frown to a slight smile. "OK, babe. We'll live for today and let tomorrow take care of itself. For now." He tucked the duvet around them. "Speaking of, the latest entry on today's agenda is a visit with Ruby."

"Ruby? The old lady with the obnoxious little dog?"

"Cosmo isn't obnoxious." Growing up, Eddie got everything he'd asked for except a dog. "Tori called your cell phone. Early as usual."

"So that's what woke you up." Kelly scooted under the covers and cuddled with Eddie. "Remind me to thank her."

Eddie kissed the top of her head. "She said Ruby might have seen the guys who broke into Lucas's apartment."

Kelly yawned. "Shouldn't she talk to the police?"

"Tori wants us to talk to her first, then tell her and Lucas what she says." Eddie closed his eyes. "I guess I should get up and make coffee." Warmth, comfort, and the nearness of Kelly changed his mind and plan. They slept through dawn and three hours into the morning, oblivious to the tribulations of rush hour traffic twenty-three floors down and along the clog and pulse of North Lake Shore Drive.

Chapter 19

Eavesdropping

Otto Hermann stared at the object of bitter disappointment on his desk. "That's it?" He glared at the men who had brought it to him. "That boludo was throwing pesos around like popcorn at pigeons." The index finger of his right hand, bent at angles from dislocations not righted, shook mere inches from the tips of their noses. "I send you out to do one simple thing." He jabbed the finger in their chests for emphasis. "One thing. And this," he pointed at the laptop, "is the best you can do?"

Rayen stopped at the sound of voices seeping between cracks in the partially open door. She flattened her back against the hallway wall and prayed. That no one had seen her. That no one had heard her. That no one inside would die today for yesterday's failure.

"The building was secure." The tail of the dragon tattoo on the forearm of the more muscled man flicked with the knot and release of his fist. "We got in, grabbed this, left the message, and got out."

Otto's lip curled under the bristles of his barely there mustache. "What the fuck good is this?"

The taller, younger man stood his ground. "That is the link to a government on the other side of the busiest border crossing in America four hours away."

77

He gestured toward the laptop. "What's on the hard drive could be worth millions."

A feral mix of greed and doubt flared and swirled in Otto's belly. He shot a wary, narrowed look at the messenger, skidded the chair away from his desk, and sat. He opened the laptop. The blank black screen image of him reflected disbelief. His thumb depressed what he assumed to be the power button. His guess was confirmed by the beep and immediate display of a red maple leaf image. He test-tapped the keyboard. "Access Denied" flashed across the screen.

"Don't turn it on!" Long-spread fingers slammed the laptop closed. "The signal can be tracked."

"So, how do we break into this thing?" Otto's simmering anger flared. "What's on this hard drive that I'd give a shit about?"

Two pairs of eyes, one human, the other inked on his arm, stared down Otto. "We won't know until we get the passcode from the person who has it. So, we bring him here."

"And then what? Kill him?"

"I don't think that would be wise."

"Why not? Who is this person?"

"A diplomat from the Canadian embassy."

Otto snorted. "Here, I make the rules. I don't recognize diplomatic immunity. What does he know about Vasquez?"

Rayen stiffened against the hallway wall.

"It's been weeks since he was in Buenos Aires asking too many questions. He left in a hurry."

"Someone tipped him off." Otto nudged the laptop with his thumbs. "What's this diplomat's name?"

"Lucas Dominguez."

Rayen bit her lip to stifle the squeal. *He's here in Chicago! Mama! I've found him!* Silently she slid along the wall, inch by painstaking inch until the worn heel of her shoe touched nothing. She backed through the opening and crouched in a dark closet hiding place she knew well.

He's here, mama. A bus ride away. Tears of relief spilled from the pools in her eyes. Fear obliterated the onset of joy. *That bastardo listens to no one. If they bring him here, he'll die. I won't let that happen! I've got to warn him!* Rayen's planned method and escape route adjusted to a new strategy and local destination. She hugged her knees and held her breath at the approach of heavy footsteps.

78

"H-h-how are we going to g-g-get Dominguez h-here?" Rayen didn't recognize the stuttering speaker on the other side of the wall. "W-we can't j-just waltz into the embassy and t-t-take him hostage." She winced at the harsh crack of flesh slapping flesh.

"Idiot!" That voice she knew. Bastardo! "Set a trap. Use the Vasquez bitch as bait. He'll come. Make it happen. Fuck this up, and I'll cut you up."

The footsteps resumed and began to fade. Rayen listened. Waited. She didn't dare move until Hermann had the last word.

"The cops won't find all your parts!" he shouted.

Rayen straightened at the slam of the door.

Chapter 20

Cool Reception

Paul grabbed the top file from their shared wire basket pile and rolled his chair around the desk. "Thing didn't earn an honorable mention in the ME's report on the bodies buried at the fiber optic installation site."

Jim opened the file, and low whistled through his teeth. "Three others did. Plenty of parts."

"But not one complete person."

"This is some sick shit. Dismemberment is all these murders have in common."

"Like this case. Puzzle pieces that don't fit together." Paul swiveled in his chair and rolled it back behind his desk. "I can almost recite every word in that report from memory, and still, I've got nothing."

"Because there's nothing here but DNA. Mud but no footprints. Dried blood but no fingerprints." Jim picked at the grunge in his coffee cup. "I couldn't see shit on that surveillance video from the apartment building either. The camera was too far away, and the footage was blurred."

Paul nodded in agreement. "Yeah, except for the one with the limp, those two could fit the description of just about any mug in a lineup." He glanced at the open door to the far corner office and faked a cough into his fist. "Here comes the forty-ninth parallel cavalry," he warned his partner. Sergeant Talbot trailed the pack behind two men and a woman, all wearing suits and solemn expressions. "Ross. Callaway." Their CO motioned them to join the procession to an open room reserved for private briefings and interrogations.

"Can't say I didn't warn you," Jim said.

Paul stood. "Senior officer first."

"I'm thinking about early retirement."

"Yeah? How soon?"

"End of shift." Jim swung the suit jacket from the back of his chair and slipped the sleeves over his rumpled white shirt. The rolled-up tie in his pocket stayed where it was.

"Detectives Jim Ross and Paul Callaway." Sergeant Talbot closed the door behind her officers. "RCMP Inspector Donald Freeland, Agent Lea Cartier of the Canadian Security Intelligence Service, and Craig Perdue from the Consulate General's office."

Handshakes didn't warm the greeting by a single degree. The meeting came to order seconds after all were seated in stiff chairs at the aged wooden rectangular table marred by years of use and occasional abuse.

"Detectives, I have assured our colleagues the department will fully cooperate for the duration of this investigation," the sergeant said.

"Let's be clear." Agent Cartier leaned forward on her elbows and forearms. Hands folded on the table. Brown eyes focused on Jim and Paul. "Our interests concern the continued safety of a Canadian citizen and the return of the laptop taken from Mr. Dominguez. The retrieval and theft of any information stored on the hard drive constitute a serious and potentially hostile breach of national security."

"Don't you think the specifics of this case are rather odd?" Jim said. "Why this apartment? Why that car? The perps had to know exactly who they were going after. Then there's the matter of the threat left on the door. There can't be too many diplomats from Canada living in Chicago who would know Argentine lingo."

Inspector Freeland's square jaw twitched. "We are aware of those facts and fully intend to pursue the answers to those questions."

"Well, if I were leading this investigation, I'd start with your diplomat. What's on that laptop that whoever took it wanted? They could have walked out with anything." Jim shrugged. "Just saying."

"I've already spoken with Lucas," Craig Perdue clarified in a French accent. "At this point, he is as much in the dark about who might have done this as we all are."

"I'm not so sure about that," Jim responded. "That's not the read I had the night of the break-in."

The three foreign officials exchanged unreadable glances. Agent Cartier scooted the chair away from the table and stood. Her colleagues did the same. "We appreciate your cooperation."

"Detectives." Inspector Freeland nodded acknowledgment.

"Thank you, Sergeant Talbot," said the consulate representative. "We'll be in touch."

"I'll show you out." The sergeant raised an eyebrow as she passed Jim and Paul. They watched through the glass separating the interrogation room and the cluster of workstations.

"Way to kick the myth of the big friendly country to the curb," Jim said as their CO host and guests maneuvered through the maze to the elevator.

"They probably don't like our beer, either." Paul stopped his partner at the open door. "How much detail did you put in that report?"

"As in, what?"

"Names of witnesses."

"Other than the diplomat's girlfriend and the neighbor who called the super about the noises in his apartment, there weren't any."

"What about Cecily and the PIs?"

Jim frowned. "Who?"

Paul grinned. "You are a piece of work, Ross."

"I have no idea what you're talking about." Jim turned off the overhead lights and closed the interrogation room door. "Just doin' my job."

Chapter 21

Dragon Tattoo

Brittle leaves blown in the first real blast announcing winter's approach spilled out of clogged corners in the building's brick and concrete entryway. Kelly kicked at the debris of summer's end around her ankles and folded her arms under the brass buttons of the black wool coat she wore.

"Hurry up! I'm freezing!"

Eddie pressed the call button a third time. "Maybe Ruby isn't home."

"Well, if she doesn't answer in two seconds, I'm leaving."

"Hello?" The tentative voice of age and uncertainty crackled and broke higher with the question.

"Hello, Ruby? It's Eddie and Kelly. We met you in the parking lot. We're friends of Lucas."

"Oh, yes. Didn't I see you here last night?"

Eddie and Kelly exchanged glances. "We were here. We'd like to talk to you about what else you might have seen."

The secure lock buzzed and clicked. Eddie opened the door. "After you, babe."

Ruby stood at the door to her apartment. Cosmo yipped and bounced on his paws.

"Hey there, little buddy." Eddie bent and scratched the puffs of groomed white fur behind the tiny dog's ears.

"Cosmo, come back inside with mama." Ruby stepped back. "How nice to see you both again. Please, let me take your coats."

"That's OK, Ruby," Kelly said. "I think I'll keep mine on for now."

"Oh, you poor dear. It is quite chilly today." Ruby locked the door and led them to a cozy kitchenette. "I'll make us a nice pot of hot tea."

Eddie slid a chair away from the four-seat table. "Don't go to any trouble for us, Ruby."

"Nonsense. It's no bother. I always have tea in the afternoon."

Kelly sat and spread her fingers on the vinyl tablecloth stamped with daisies identical to the pattern on the wallpaper. "Reminds me of my grandmother's kitchen," she told Eddie.

"You had a grandmother?"

The corners of her lips turned up, then down into a frown. "Of course I did."

"You haven't told me much about your family at all."

"Here we are." Ruby brought a tray of daisy-adorned china cups and saucers, a teapot, and small pitcher of milk. She poured the tea, took her cup, and sat opposite Kelly. "Have you heard from Lucas?"

"He's staying with his, uh, friend Tori."

"Oh, yes. That pretty young woman with lovely red hair. Victoria, I believe. They seem so happy together. Made for each other. Just like the two of you." Ruby poured milk into her tea. "Dating was different back in my day. Couples don't wait until marriage anymore. But that's nobody's business, really. Love is love whenever it happens." She sipped her tea and sighed. "I fell in love with my Henry on our first date. He took me to a movie. I don't remember which one it was. I was so happy just to be with him. He took my hand when the lights went down. We held hands until they came on again." Ruby drifted momentarily in the wispy tendrils of steam from her cup. "Now. What did you want to ask me?"

"Ruby, Victoria told us you saw two men at the front door last night," Kelly said.

"Indeed I did. Before going to bed every night, I check to ensure my front door is locked and the security alarm is turned on. I have a habit of looking out the peephole. That's when I saw those men. They were dressed in dark clothing. One of them was wearing a jacket. The other only had on a short sleeve t-shirt. I thought that was odd, considering it was chilly and raining. They were having trouble with the keypad. The man wearing the jacket pulled hard on the door until it opened."

"What did they do after they got in the building? Did they stop? Look around? Go to any of the main floor apartments?" Eddie asked.

"Oh, no. They walked right in past my door and down the hallway toward the stairs. Like they knew where they were going. I probably should have called the police right then. But I wasn't sure if maybe they were here to visit or check on somebody. I had to use the bathroom, and I was getting cold, so I went to my bedroom and got my robe before I checked the hallway again. Those two men practically ran out the front door. A few minutes later, I heard the glass breaking out front in the parking lot."

"Did you notice anything else unusual about these guys?" Kelly asked.

"How do you mean unusual?"

"Something that would identify them. Was one shorter than the other? Walk with a limp? Was either of them bald? Have facial hair? Body piercings or a tattoo?"

Ruby's eyes shone. Her expression brightened. "Yes! The shorter man limped. The man who wasn't wearing a jacket had a tattoo on his arm. A dragon, as I recall. Green with a long tail and a red tongue."

"You're sure about that?" Eddie asked.

"Positive. Is that helpful?"

"Yes, Ruby," he said. "That's very helpful." Eddie swallowed a mouthful of tea and glanced at his watch. "We've taken up enough of your time. Thank you so much."

"You're most welcome. Anything I can do to help Lucas. He's such a nice man." Concern knit lines around her eyes and the corners of her mouth. "Did those men steal anything from his apartment?"

"Nothing that can't be replaced." Kelly drank some tea and followed Eddie's lead. "Thanks for the tea, Ruby," she said over her shoulder.

"My pleasure. We always welcome company." Cosmo barked as the door closed on Ruby's apartment.

Ice pellets skittered across the sidewalk and parking lot. A strong gust of wind rocked the Jeep seconds after they'd buckled up. "Let's get home before this gets worse." Eddie stuck the key in the ignition and started the engine. Kelly fished her cell phone from the bottom of her bag.

"I'm calling Tori." Kelly tapped the first contact displayed.

The cell phone in Eddie's pocket buzzed. "Better double-check that number."

"I didn't call you," she said to Eddie. "Hi, Tori," Kelly spoke into the phone. "Sorry about that. Of course, I called you."

"Hello?" Eddie answered.

"Eddie. Lucas here."

Well, that's weird. "Hey, we just left Ruby's place. Kelly is on the phone with Tori now. Maybe we can get together and ..."

Lucas cut in. "I need to speak with you. It's very important. What I have to say has to stay between us for now. Please, don't tell Kelly. I don't want Victoria to know what I plan to do if you agree to help me."

Really weird. "OK. You got a time and place in mind?"

"The café in One Prudential Plaza. Can you meet me tomorrow morning around seven-thirty?"

"No problem. See you then."

"Thank you."

I've got a bad feeling about this. Eddie pocketed the phone. *I hope he's not thinking about going rogue in Chicago. What do I say to stop him if he is?* He tuned out Kelly's conversation with Tori. Questions he couldn't answer and the drive home at the front end of Monday evening rush hour on slippery pavement consumed his concentration.

Chapter 22

Passionate Confession

Waves of sensory comfort folded around Lucas. He closed his eyes and relished the moment of calm. Warmth absorbed and chased the chill of late November. The snap of oil and sizzle of beef browned and braised in a hot pan. The savory scent of freshly chopped carrots, potatoes, and red onions simmered in garlic and herbs.

"Lucas? Did you get my message, love?"

The sound of his lover's voice. Lucas opened his eyes. Victoria. *My beautiful one.* Crystal clear green eyes like delicate glass cherished as rare by an artisan of antiquities. Look, but do not touch. Break, and you pay. Silky ivory skin as tempting to the taste as cream. Deep, provocative dimples in cheeks blushed pink by the kitchen stove heat. Ginger curls tumbled to shoulders laid bare by the loose fit drape of a neckline and top over breasts that fit perfectly in his palms. Leggings clung to curves he knew by heart.

She stripped his reason away.

"I just put dinner in the oven. When the storm started, I canceled our reservations." She rose up on toes to heels covered by flat black slippers. Her arms circled his neck. "I hope you don't mind the change in plans."

"Not at all." His hands stroked her. His lips met hers in a sweet, sustained press of urgency held constant as he carried her. He lay with her on the bed and warmed her with his caress. Undressed her slowly and whispered his desire for each revealed part of her. She moaned and writhed at his touch. His lips moved between her breasts from one to the other. Breath on the dampness from his tongue heightened her arousal. His fingers on and in her stimulated more from within.

"Lucas." She tugged at his belt.

"Patience, mon amour." The trail of his lips and tongue led to the place where his fingers had been. The circle stroke of his thumbs and heels of his palms opened her thighs. He moaned with the taste of her. Tori's cry rumbled from deep within her. Her back arched. Her fists gripped peaked tufts of comforter down.

He smiled, pleased at the power of the release he'd given her. He removed what he wore and stood over her. Admired her. Waited for her to be ready for him.

"Lucas," she breathed. The fire in her eyes flamed. His fire for her raged. He plunged into her. Rolled with the squeeze of her thighs at his hips. Rocked as her legs wrapped around him. Surrendered to the heat of sensual stimulation and visceral passion. Groaned in sated pleasure. Collapsed beside her in a cool-down tremble.

"Victoria." He whispered her name like a prayer. "Me pierdo en ti, mi amor. I haven't said those words to a woman since Adriana."

Tori nestled under his arm. Her fingernails played with the hair on his chest. "What do the words mean?"

"I lose myself in you, my love." He brought her hand to his lips. "Me pierdo en ti mi amor," he repeated.

"But you were just a boy then."

"The boy had been infatuated. I was seventeen when Adriana left me. The man knew he was in love."

"You told me you got married. What about your wife?"

Lucas paused a moment to remember the woman he'd married. "Barbara was a good woman. I met her at university. She was in her last year of law school. I was finishing up my MBA. Our marriage was comfortable. We had a good life together. I was devastated when she died. She'd been an important part of my life for over twenty years. I cared deeply for her as she did for me. I loved her. But she was not the love of my life. I was certain that intense love, that once-in-a-lifetime passion, that connection beyond reason, was lost to me. Then I found you."

Lucas rolled to his side and looked into her eyes. His fingers stroked and parted her hair. His hand cupped her cheek. "The consulate is concerned for my safety. I may be recalled home before I was scheduled to leave here. I wanted you to know so you wouldn't think I'd left you again without an explanation. Without telling you where I was going or why I had to go."

Tori blinked. A tear trailed from the corner of her eye. "You're going back to Canada?"

He gently caught the tear in his fingertips. "Victoria. Listen to me. This is not how or where I planned to tell you. We were supposed to enjoy a candlelit dinner and a fine bottle of champagne. I would hold your hand like this," his fingers curled around her left hand, "and I would get down on my knee and ask you to marry me. A proper proposal as every woman deserves. That will come later. But for now, know this. I love you beyond reason. I want you with me for the rest of our lives. When the day comes that I have to leave, I will go back to Montreal and wait for you to join me. If that is what you want, too."

"Oh, Lucas." Her sob startled him. Her deep-dimpled smile delighted him. "I love you so much. Of course, I'll come to Montreal. I'd go wherever to be with you. Yes, I will marry you. I can't wait to be your wife. But." Her dimples disappeared with the frown. "What if you find Adriana?"

"Mon amour." His lips softly kissed hers. "My love for Adriana was real. I was young. We were young. Life has changed us. Neither of us is the same person we were when we said goodbye." He took her hand and held it firmly in his. "This is who I am now. What I feel for you now is real." He pressed her hand to his chest over his heart. "Je t'aime. Te quiero."

"I love you." They spoke together in a language and vow shared.

Chapter 23

Desperation

Eddie wasn't fooled by the clear sky at sunrise. Shifting winds off Lake Michigan could turn the weather from fair to fickle in seconds, regardless of the season. He dressed in layers. Duty to a client battled the urge to take off everything and snuggle naked against Kelly, arouse her sweetly and slowly, and make love until exhaustion or coffee, whichever came first.

I hope I don't regret this decision. He left a note under her cell phone and descended in the elevator from their home at the top to the lobby attended by employees of the Emerson family empire. The taxi he'd hired waited under the canopy. "One Pru Plaza," Eddie told the driver. *Damn! If it weren't for the holidays, I'd hate December.* He shivered and blew hot breath into the gloves on his hands.

Barren tree limbs dripped nature's pre-season tinsel. Ice coated every surface untouched by tires or pedestrians. Concrete glared—a take it slow warning. Eddie generously tipped the driver, who'd dodged snarled traffic and followed city trucks spewing salt to get him to the café on time.

Lucas waved and motioned him to a far corner table. Eddie noticed the cups and carafe. Good man but not necessarily a good sign.

"Good morning, Eddie." Lucas poured the cups full. "Thanks for meeting me on such short notice."

"Comes with the job description." Eddie hung his coat on the back of the chair and sat. "What have you got in mind?"

"I like that about you." Lucas wrapped his hands around the cup. "You get right to the point. So, I will as well. The assistant to the Consulate General met with Detective Ross, his partner, and their commanding officer yesterday. The theft of my laptop is being investigated by CSIS, my country's agency similar to your CIA, as a potential security risk to the government of Canada. The RCMP is also involved because of the possible threat to my safety. I may be recalled to Ottawa at any time. I've been thinking about what your partner Cecily said about Rayen sending the mate cup as a forwarding message. I fear we're running out of time to find Adriana's daughter." Lucas's dark-eyed gaze hardened with determination. "I want you to take me to where you and Kelly saw Rayen. I'm going to search for her and bring her back to Canada with me."

Eddie choked on his sip of coffee. "That's not a good idea. Go in unarmed and without police backup? It's way too dangerous. Criminals that peddle human flesh for profit will do anything to keep what's theirs."

"Then what can we do?" Determination shifted to wild-eyed desperation. "I can't sit by and do nothing! Rayen is in danger, and I have to get her to safety. I owe that to Camila and Adriana."

"I get that. And I admire you for it. But there has to be a better way." Eddie drummed his fingers on the table. "How about we scale back this plan? Take it one step at a time."

"How do you mean?"

"Figure out a way to get a message to Rayen that won't land us in the line of fire. Sorry, man, but Kelly has to be in on this. Cecily, too. She was a Chicago PD detective and Jim's partner, so she knows how he works. And she's a forensic psychologist. An expert witness the district attorney relies on to prosecute criminal court cases. We need her expertise."

"But no police." The desperation in his eyes shifted back to stern resolve.

Eddie raised his hands, palms forward in a show of surrender. "Not unless the going gets weird."

Lucas took his time drinking the coffee. Eddie waited out the anxious moments between mouthfuls of rich dark roast.

"What you say makes sense." Lucas lifted the carafe and refilled their cups.

"So, you're OK with that?" Eddie asked.

"For now." The diplomat's eyes shone with force from within that stopped Eddie's rebuttal cold.

***

Warmed air in the penthouse couldn't chase the chill that seeped from behind and beneath Kelly's closed home office door.

"Babe?" Eddie knocked on the door. "I'm back from my run." He glanced around the four thousand square feet of mostly open floor plan. Doors to other private spaces, including the bedroom they shared, were open. Not a single dirty dish cluttered the unoccupied kitchen. He knocked again. "Kel? Did you have breakfast?"

The door opened. Her icy stare made him shiver more than stepping out into the morning cold. "You lied." She closed the door.

He heard the lock click.

"C'mon, Kel. This is ridiculous."

"So is the excuse for your disappearing act." The heavy wood on hinges didn't muffle Kelly's response. He heard her loud and clear. "You don't run in the morning anymore. You only run once a day, and you'd never run the morning after an ice storm."

I'm busted. She knows me too well. That's what I get for being in love with my best friend. "I'm sorry about the note. Give me a chance to tell you my reason for writing it." He counted to ten. "You didn't answer my wrong question." *Think of an offer she can't refuse.* "I'll make buttermilk pancakes."

The door opened. Kelly still wore her robe over her pajamas. The toes of blue suede moccasins peeked out underneath. "We don't have any buttermilk."

"But we do have blueberries."

She side-stepped around and passed him. "I'll make coffee." They went through the opening motions of meal preparation in strained silence broken by Kelly's to-the-point inquiry.

"So where were you, and why wasn't I invited?"

Eddie dropped ladles of pancake batter into a hot-oiled skillet. The powerful fan in the stainless-steel hood over the multi-burner cooktop sucked away the subtle smoke but not the delicious scent. His stomach growled. "Lucas wanted to meet without the women folk."

"The women folk?" Kelly punctuated the question with an indignant squeak.

He laughed and caught the spatula she tossed. "Relax. I wasn't a fan at first. But I'm glad you and Tori weren't there. It gave me a chance to talk him out of doing something crazy and into a more doable and less dicey plan."

Eddie flipped and served plates of golden browned breakfast. He shared the details of his café conversation with Lucas between bites and sips of black coffee. Kelly choked into the napkin she'd used to wipe melted butter and sticky maple syrup from her lips.

"He wanted to do what?!"

"Yeah, that was pretty much my reaction." Eddie pushed away an empty plate on the kitchen island marble. "Getting him to stand down was relatively easy. The tough part comes next."

"How to get a message to Rayen." Kelly sat back and swiveled in the custom-made bar stool. "We have to find her first. Or at least narrow down the most likely location."

"What about his laptop?"

Kelly shook her head. "It must be an older model. I'm unsure, but I'm guessing the signal can only be tracked if the laptop is turned on."

"Then that's it. That's the message we need to get to her."

"Lucas is here. Turn on the laptop."

"Exactly."

"That's assuming the men that Ruby saw broke into his apartment and took the laptop to where Rayen is and that she's seen and has access to said laptop."

"You got any better ideas?"

"Frankly, no, I don't. Maybe Cecily does." Kelly cleared and stacked the dishes they'd used in the dishwasher. "I'll see if she's free to meet us."

"Invite her over." Eddie caught her in his arms and nuzzled her neck. "I'll make lunch or dinner. Or we can order out for delivery."

"My, but you're feeling generous."

"And amorous." He slipped his hands under her open robe. His arms circled her.

"Phone first." She kissed him soft to deep. He groaned and reached for more. "Sex later." She spun out of his grasp and retreated to her home-based workspace.

"Not much later." Eddie retraced his steps through her office door. He spotted the cell phone on the floor. "What's up? No signal?" He picked up the phone. "Or does this battery need a recharge too?"

Kelly's fingers rapid-tapped the keyboard of the open laptop on her desk. "The laptop is on." She pointed at the screen. "If we've got the clues right, Sherlock, that's where Rayen is." Kelly typed in the screen print command to save the image. "Now all we have to do is figure out how to deliver that message." She took the phone from him and called Cecily.

"Is that all?" Eddie stared at the intersection to their west and south, bordering the malicious side of Marshall Square.

Chapter 24

Spidey Senses

Jim walked the city's blocks along North Western from Cortez to Thomas. The deceptive afternoon sun wasn't warming him. Salt mixed with kitty litter scattered on the sidewalk crunched under his shoes.

Paul stood in front of the corner tobacco business. Head down. The pen in his hand moved over the pages of his partner's ever-present notebook.

"Tell me again why we're here. Last time I looked at a city of Chicago map, the west side of Ukrainian Village ain't in our wheelhouse."

"The MO on the body found in the alley last night might be." Paul crossed the street. Jim followed him down the narrow path between the backs of businesses and apartment buildings. Closed and open garages. Some with cars, others empty and waiting for the end of the day. A few backyards were cordoned off by wrought iron and cedar wood. A black and white spotted dog snapped and growled a warning from the corralled inner sanctum of chain link where Paul stopped. "Neighbors called animal control on this dude's owner. The body was in a dumpster over there." He pointed with his pen to a rectangular area of exposed concrete that had obviously been sheltered from the storm.

"Parts missing?"

"Hands, feet, and head."

"Another DNA ID. Witnesses?"

"Not a one."

Jim glanced over his shoulder at the growling dog. "Too bad he can't talk." A sudden gust from the north blew discarded pop cans and assorted trash down the manmade tunnel. Jim shoved his ungloved hands into his coat pockets. "It's not our case, Callaway. So again, I have to ask. Why are we here?"

"The more I read and reread the report, the more I got the feeling that something was missed." Paul pocketed his notebook and pen. "Chalk it up to the ice storm, shift change, or not enough uniforms on the duty roster."

"That's good enough for me. Let's walk it out until your spidey sense is satisfied. But can we pick up the pace? I'm freezing my ass off." Jim both cursed and cheered the stiff wind that kept the stench under the lifted dumpster and garbage can lids from lingering in his nostrils. He opened and quickly dropped the lid on the third dumpster checked less than a block away from the one that had been removed as evidence.

"Jesus." Jim's vision blurred. The buzz in his head gained volume. He braced the heels of his palms on bent knees and willed the spin to recede. "Callaway," he called out.

"You OK, Ross?" Paul steadied his partner. "You need a bus?"

Jim filled his lungs with air and let it out slowly. "I'm alright. You were right. There's another body in there. At least this one is whole."

Paul slowly let go of Jim and raised the dumpster's lid. "Oh, my God." He closed the metal tomb and kicked a dent in the can next to it.

"Yeah." Jim straightened up. "Just a boy."

Chapter 25

Paco's Demise

Rayen couldn't concentrate. Worry had short-circuited her ability to accurately count stacks of cash on sight.

Cold through the cracks in bricks and mortar around single-paned windows seeped into her bones. Rayen flexed stiff fingers and stared at the blank ledger sheet. Her lack of progress on the daily profit numbers would anger Otto. It didn't take much to set him off. The respite of his absence could end at any moment.

Shafts of noon-hour sunlight bore through the hole between buildings to the floor of the narrow pit of the alley below. Rayen calculated the number of dust motes in a single golden beam tinged blue by the winter sky. Blessed calm abruptly ended with a scream.

Rayen rose from her desk and turned in to the full force of a fist at her sternum. Her knees touched down hard on the bare floor. She crumpled in a reflexive hug.

"You bitch!" A young Latina reeking of hairspray, drug store cologne, and sex breathed venom into the open sore of her victim's debilitation. "You killed him!" She knotted her fingers into a cluster of knuckles not intended for prayer and slammed both fists into the back of Rayen's skull. "He was my only friend, and you took him from me!"

Rayen folded into a fetal position of self-preservation and fought to stay conscious. Breath returned in short spurts through the 'oh' her lips formed. Her attacker's sobs rattled in excruciating waves of physical and emotional pain. The outline of her face floated in images of distorted shadow and color.

"He brought me flowers, root beer, and a chocolate bunny at Easter." She blew her nose and flicked the snot away with her thumb. "He sang to me in Spanish and fetched me ice when the trick I had to turn got too rough." Her face contorted in agony released. "He was a good kid. Do you know what he did with the money you paid him to deliver that package? He bought me this bracelet."

Rayen blinked to focus on the silver heart-shaped charm dangling on a silver chain. She struggled to squelch the lightning bolts behind her eyes and in her chest. "Paco es muerto?" she managed above a whisper.

"Si! Mi Pacito se ha ido." A fresh trail of tears, streaked dark ribbons of makeup applied in copious amounts and colors to eyelashes, lids, and cheeks. "My boy is gone."

"How? Who?"

"Don't play stupid, chica! You had to know. Otto watches what you do. He has eyes everywhere! You cross him, you pay. When he's done with you, you die." She stood tall in black spandex on thin legs that trembled from the effort. "I pray for an end. I pray my time and yours will come soon." The tall skinny heels on her too-big shoes clacked with her exit across cracked linoleum tiles.

Tears compounded her headache. Sobs worsened Rayen's struggle to breathe. *Lo siento, Paco. I am so sorry.* Contrition reverted quickly to rage and an oath for vengeance.

We will come for you, Bastardo!

Chapter 26

The Chase

The bus rolled to a stop on the street in a neighborhood Cecily vowed she'd never set foot in again. Squat commercial buildings blended in tableau of typical Chicago brick and mortar with single-family residences that likely housed multiple unrelated tenants. Patched sidewalks connected with newer cut curbs and beaten down streets marred by crooked mini-crater crevices and muddy water potholes. The canopy over the bodega's door hadn't weathered the storms and seasons well. Cecily remembered the red as less faded. But the windows behind the wrought iron bars were just as dirty. Nothing much changes when there's nothing to lose.

But there had been loss here. Caleb Gillespie lost his life. Kelly lost her brother. Memories of the crushing defeat that had robbed Detective Cecily Vosh of a conviction and a career collided with doubts of the present-day purpose to continue.

What am I doing here? This is one fucked up plan.

***

"I have to be the one to deliver the message." Cecily sank into the big butter-soft leather chair opposite Kelly and Eddie who'd settled on the matching sectional sofa. She plopped wool sock-covered feet in the center of the chair's oversized matching footstool. Ambient light in the penthouse complemented the clear night view of Lake Michigan framed by floor-to-ceiling glass. "A sista of color blends in with the natives. You my friends, do not." Cecily sniffed at the chardonnay in the long-stemmed glass she cradled in her palm. *Smells too rich to even sip.* "Isn't having wine around too much temptation to fall off the wagon?"

Eddie squeezed juice from a slice of lime into his glass of mineral water. "We only keep a bottle around for guests. Whiskey was always my poison of choice. Wine reminds me of the soirees on the family compound in Connecticut. I poured so much of it for my mother Felicity's cheek patting and pinching guests that I can't stand the smell of the stuff."

"Fair enough." Cecily sipped and tasted butterscotch in the wine. *Poor rich guy doesn't know what he's missing.* "Another major advantage in my favor is a license to carry."

"Can't argue with that," Eddie agreed.

"So why don't either or both of you have one? A license to carry, I mean. Every other PI that I know does."

Kelly frowned over the rim of her glass. *How could the cop who'd failed to find Caleb's killer ask that question?* "I don't like guns. And I don't like you going in alone and us with no police backup."

Cecily shrugged. "Piece of cake. I get off the bus, take my sweet time walking to the address, check out the building, and look for Rayen. When I see her, I hand off the message in the bag Lucas gave us, the one that had the mate cup in it, walk back to the bodega, and take the next bus out. If I don't see her within a reasonable amount of time, I'll get out of there the same way."

"But what if this doesn't go down as planned?" Kelly's concern for her friend showed in the wrinkles between her eyebrows. "What if you're spotted? What if you can't get out?"

"We'll have our cell phones," Eddie said. "I'll be parked in the Jeep a safe distance away but close enough to get to Cecily in a hurry if I have to," Eddie said.

"Oh, so you're taking my car."

"I'm certainly not taking Petula."

"You can take my car," Cecily said. "Nobody's going to look twice at a Camaro with rusted wheel wells. Hey, she's not much to look at but punch the accelerator, and there's plenty of life left in that old girl."

"So, I'll be with Eddie," Kelly said.

He shook his head. "You're staying here."

"No, I'm not."

"Yes, you are." Cecily cut off Kelly's protest. "Girlfriend, we need you to let us know if that laptop fires up again so we can confirm the location because I doubt the address is plastered on the mailbox. And, in the unlikely event this goes seriously to hell, you'll call for backup."

Kelly crossed her knee over the other and kicked out with her dangling foot. "Now, I really don't like this plan."

"Well, it's the best one we've got," Eddie said. "So, let's drink to it."

***

Cecily licked her lips. She could still taste the chardonnay. With the bag slung over her shoulder, she shook off hesitation and got off the bus.

The smell of diesel fumes from departed mass transit aggravated nausea brought on by a flood of memories. Caleb's body—buried fifteen years in a north-side neighborhood grave—splayed in the street. Eyes set, spark gone, torso and limbs contorted in violent death. Blood spilled from an unnatural dent in his skull. Cecily's knuckles had banged on dozens of doors that never opened. Questions asked when faces did appear were mostly ignored. Others answered with lies that led nowhere. Unproven suspicions were confirmed by eyebrows that arched and lips that twitched at the mention of a name. The closer Cecily got to the truth, the more it slipped out of her reach.

She walked the bodega's aisles and scanned cases and corners for security cameras in full view and possible hiding places. The dark-skinned middle-aged guy behind the counter with more hair on his forearms than his head took the twenty-dollar bill she handed him to buy a chocolate bar. His rise-and-fall pitch wolf whistle trailed her exit.

Baby doll-sized brown eyes of the girl child in a coat held together by safety pins as button substitutes stared at the candy Cecily offered. She snatched it. Ripped off the wrapper and ran away as though fearful Cecily might change her mind. Shadows between buildings and down alleys played peek-a-boo with shafts of the late afternoon sun. Cecily walked an apparent random path toward a deliberate destination.

The building where she might find Rayen had no physical address. Cecily wasn't surprised. She'd studied the available online maps from every possible angle. She passed by on purpose, circled the block, and texted Eddie. All good so far. Going in closer. Streetlights flickered on in the waning hour of daylight. Cecily rounded the corner into the laneway behind the unmarked building. The holstered Glock on her belt rode at her hip, accessible yet hidden under her coat.

Movement on the interior side of a grimy, below-street-level window distracted and captured her attention. Cropped, thick black hair traced the jawline of a heart-shaped face. She paced the near-empty room with no apparent purpose. Cecily squatted and swiped at the window's grime with her coat sleeve. Tapped on the glass. The pacing stopped. She came to the window. Dark eyes focused on the intruder at her eye level.

"What are you doing here?"

Cecily pivoted on the balls of her feet, ready to rise, fight or run. Round brown eyes stared into hers. A sliver of light beamed from overhead glanced off the shiny head of a safety pin under her chin. "I've got something to give to my friend in there."

The girl's eyes rolled and narrowed. "She doesn't have any friends. Nobody here does."

"She does." Cecily held the bag to the window and motioned a signal she hoped Rayen would understand. "This is for her." The rumble of male voices nearby triggered an alarm in Cecily that years away from law enforcement had not silenced. "Can you give this to her for me?" Cecily reached into her coat pocket for the change from the candy she'd bought at the bodega and shoved the paper bills into the girl's hand. The girl took the bag.

Stiff hinges creaked with the opening swing of the building's back door. Cecily ran for the nearest cover of darkness. Her outstretched fingers scraped mortar as she crept close to the bricks. The scuff and scramble of quick heavy footsteps echoed in the urban cavern. She fumbled in her coat pocket for the cell phone. "Eddie!"

"Where are you?" he answered.

"About ten feet from the end of the alley."

"I'm close. Stay there!"

"I will if I can." The footsteps got closer. "Don't hang up! I may have to run." The scream she heard didn't sound human. Cecily flinched at the pounce of a feral cat on the twitching rodent in its claws. She crouched beneath the iron steps of a fire escape. Car doors slammed nearby. A fired-up engine revved. Cold sweat snaked down her spine. "C'mon, Eddie!"

"I'm here!"

Cecily dodged broken glass and a crushed pizza box to the end of the alley and the open passenger's side door of her Camaro. Eddie swerved into traffic before she was buckled in.

"What happened?" he asked.

"Long story, I don't know yet." Cecily slumped in the seat and glanced in the side mirror. "Short story, we may have company real soon."

Eddie winced at the flash of headlights in the rear-view mirror. "If the low rider kissing the back bumper is any indication, company has arrived." Brakes screeched on the delivery truck, cut off by Eddie's sudden left turn maneuver. The driver screamed obscenities at the black sedan that tailed the Chevy. Eddie floored the accelerator and cranked the steering wheel right at the next corner. Tires under the driver's side whined. The other pair briefly left the pavement. He swore as the headlights flashed again. "Fuckers."

Cecily clutched her cell phone. "Fuck this. I'm calling for backup." The unexpected violent skid and spin of Eddie's attempt at escape bounced the phone out of her hand.

"What is the nature of your emergency?" The connected voice of the dispatcher spoke from the mat at Cecily's feet.

"Gun!" Eddie shouted and stomped on the accelerator. The Camaro careened down a side street. The blast from behind shattered the rear window.

"Shots fired!" Cecily recovered the phone and pulled the Glock from her holster. Words on the street sign at the next corner froze like a snapshot in her viewfinder. "Northbound on South Oakley cross street Coulter and Twenty-fifth!"

The driver steered the sedan around to Cecily's right. The barrel of a gun appeared in the lowered window behind the driver. "Floor it!" Cecily yelled.

"I am!" Eddie screamed over the wail of approaching sirens. A lit-up marked squad blocked the major intersection at Cermak Road less than a handful of city blocks ahead. The pursuer dropped back and veered to the left. Eddie cut in on the right lane opening. "Hang on!" Eddie pumped the brakes.

The Camaro skidded sideways and jumped the curb. A front tire blew. The side of Cecily's car missed an unforgiving impact with a fire hydrant by inches.

The black sedan copied the spin and circled back on a parallel course. "Get down!" Cecily grabbed Eddie's shoulders. The Camaro quivered with the shot buried in metal above the rust in the rear wheel well. The car rocked with the whoosh of squads speeding past in pursuit of the sedan.

Cecily peeked cautiously over the dashboard and turned the key in the ignition. The engine shut down with a shudder.

Eddie didn't move. "Is the coast clear?"

Cecily looked out and around into the eerie calm. Anyone who may have been out on the street or sidewalks had apparently taken cover. She holstered her sidearm and sat up. "Appears so." She jumped at the tap on the glass next to her right ear. A colored strobe flashed in the darkness. The face in the window belonged to an EMT. "Everybody OK in there?" the medic asked.

"I am." She poked Eddie. "You OK?"

"Yeah. I think so." He straightened and frowned. "But I really need to change my boxers."

Chapter 27

Clear Direction

The caller that interrupted his rare opportunity to sleep in was not who Jim expected. He considered ignoring the cell phone ring. Let the message go to voicemail. *It could be Bonnie.* He'd encouraged his daughter and only child to work smart in college and avoid all-night study sessions during senior year finals week with her career goals set on medicine. Don't worry so much, Papa Bear, she said. Just wish me luck. Jim silently cursed his decision to answer.

"It's our day off, Callaway," he grumbled. "I don't intend to spend it with you."

"Hear me out. You may change your mind."

"I doubt it." Jim rolled onto his back. "Have your way with Betty."

"It's Becca, and she hasn't come home yet. She's at work. Third shift at Rush Memorial ER."

Jim yawned. "Why did I need to know that?"

"Because she just called and told me a cop is in ICU, a Latino gang banger is in traction, three others left in handcuffs, and Eddie and Cecily Vosh were treated and released."

"Oh, fuck." Jim covered his face with a pillow. "Just kill me now."

"What did you say?" Paul asked.

"Nothing." Jim tossed the pillow at the headboard and swung his legs over the side of the mattress. "We might as well go in before Sarge calls us in."

"Exactly why I called you first," Paul said. "See you in thirty."

"Great," Jim muttered at the disconnection. "There go the plans for today that I hadn't made."

***

The grey dawn was breaking on their arrival at the station house. Sergeant Talbot motioned them into her office. "Thank you for coming in on your day off, detectives. Close the door." She pointed the tip of her pen at a pair of new grass-green leather back and seat-cushioned side chairs. Pieces of the protective plastic they'd been delivered in clung to the legs. "Have a seat."

The pressed collar of Paul's shirt rested under smooth skin without a missed whisker. His suit appeared fresh from the dry cleaners. Sergeant Talbot presented as news conference ready for live on-camera questions from a room full of reporters. Jim shined his shoes on the backs of his pants legs and buttoned his jacket to cover the wrinkled shirt. *How the hell can the two of them look so damn fresh this early in the morning?* He gritted his teeth to stifle a yawn.

"How is the officer in ICU?" Paul asked.

"Doing well after surgery," their CO responded. "She'll be moved to a room in the ward tomorrow." The sergeant handed over copies of the incident report. "Sergeant Melrose is taking the lead on the investigation."

"It's his jurisdiction, and the mutts are in his lockup." Jim rubbed the day-old growth on his chin. "Anything else on the body parts and the dead kid?"

"The boy has been identified as thirteen-year-old Paco Sanchez. The paper trail on him is spotty and mostly illegal. Seasonal farm work. On and off immigration's radar. Most likely recruited into the human trafficking begging and peddling rings," she said.

"Small-time stuff," Jim said.

"Looks that way," said Sergeant Talbot.

"Then why kill him and stuff his body in a dumpster a block away from another DNA ID case?" Paul asked.

"He must have done something that got the ring manager's attention." Jim slid the report back on his CO's desk. "So why are we at the table on a South Side case from Melrose's house?"

The sergeant folded her hands on the report file and looked directly at Jim. "You know the wild cards. You have history with Eddie Emerson and Cecily Vosh. She called dispatch and reported shots fired. They and most likely Mr. Emerson's PI partner are in this up to their noses. I want to know how and why and if last night's incident is in any way connected to the Canadian diplomat and the missing laptop the RCMP and CSIS want recovered yesterday."

"We're on it, Sarge." Jim stood. Paul was already at the door. Sergeant Talbot called them back. "The ME identified the owners of the body parts buried in the utility trench. All gang members from our side of the line." She glanced up and pointed the tip of the pen in her hand at the door. "Put the pieces together, detectives."

Paul grabbed a set of keys to an unmarked car. "So, where do we start?"

"At the source," Jim replied. "Time to roust some PIs out of their bed in Gold Coast luxury."

Chapter 28

Penthouse Drama

Eddie's lingering annoyance at the hurry up and wait, poke and prod, question and answer, police and emergency room, procedural marathon robbed him of a night's sleep. Though exhausted, he paced the penthouse long after Kelly and Cecily had gone to bed.

Kelly invited Cecily to stay when their ordeal wrapped up after midnight. "But what about Cornelius?"

"He's a cat, Kelly," Cecily said. "Cats take care of themselves. He's got food and a litter box. He'll be fine. We're all trashed, but I'm too buzzed to fall asleep. And I'm famished."

Cecily snacked on a chunk of salami on rye and relayed the details from the chocolate bar at the bodega to eye contact with Rayen.

"Did she get the bag and the note?" Kelly asked.

"While I can't say for sure since I had to retreat quickly to save my ass, I'm pretty sure Rayen got the message. I know she saw the bag. Any idea what's in the note?"

"Nope," Kelly said. "Lucas wrote it for her eyes only. He agreed to our plan to ask Rayen to locate and turn on the laptop." She glanced up at Eddie closing the fridge door, and lightly squeezed his knee on his return to the kitchen island stool beside her. "You've been quiet since we left the hospital. You OK?"

"Yeah, I'm fine," Eddie said. "Just pissed."

"About what?" Kelly asked.

"I should have seen this coming. It wasn't the best plan I've ever come up with. The outcome sure told that story in all caps and exclamation marks." He poured glasses of milk all around. "Sorry about your car," he said to Cecily.

"Oh, forget that. The insurance company will probably total it. I'll see if they'll let me have it for junk and turn it over to my main man Jake. Best mechanic and body work dude in the business."

Eddie had showered and tried to sleep. He gave up around the pre-dawn hour when he knew Tori would be awake.

"Oh, Eddie!" Tori didn't bother with hello. "I just heard about that on the news. Are you and Cecily alright?"

"We got banged up a bit, and her car is a wreck. It could have been much worse. Any chance you and Lucas can meet with us at our place?"

"I'm sure we can. When?"

"This morning, if at all possible."

"I'll ask him and get back to you." The couple stepped off the penthouse elevator two hours later.

"Wow!" The panoramic view of Lake Michigan from the penthouse drew Tori to the great room floor-to-ceiling windows like a wide-eyed child to a multi-tier birthday cake ablaze with candy-striped candles. "Do you really live here?" She walked the room's length along the safe illusion of ledge at her feet. "How can you afford it?" Tori clapped her hand over her mouth. Her face flushed. "How rude of me!" she sputtered. "I am so sorry. That is absolutely none of my business."

"My father owns the building," Eddie said.

Tori's eyes went wide. "The whole building?! Oh!" She sighed. "There I go, putting my foot in it again."

"Well, before you don't have a leg to stand on, allow me to introduce you to the world of Edward Harcourt Emerson the Third, son of international financier Edward Harcourt Emerson the Second, who inherited everything he knows and owns from my grandfather the First. This is one of many pieces of prime real estate my family owns on five continents. I'm not proud of it. I've spent my life trying to distance myself from it. But extrication from wealth attached to a name isn't easy."

Lucas waded in to dispel the obvious signs of embarrassment. "I can't begin to understand the pressures this life imposes on you, Eddie. But I can empathize with the anxiety you feel. We all have burdens to carry, and we cope as best we can. Who you are and what you choose to do with your life are more important than the name given to you. Risking your life to help me find Rayen is who you are. I respect and thank you for accepting that risk."

"Words of a diplomat," Cecily whispered low in Kelly's ear.

"Or a speech from a born politician," Kelly whispered back.

The phone and line connecting the penthouse with building security jangled an alert from its perch on a narrow glass-topped table in the hallway. "Excuse me," he said to his guests, "please, sit soft." Eddie walked away from the windows and picked up what he and Kelly jokingly referred to as 'The Bat Phone'. "Yes, Bruce," he answered.

"Good morning, Mr. Emerson. Detectives Ross and Callaway are here to see you."

Eddie groaned.

"Is there a problem, sir?"

"Are they actually in the building?" Muffled sounds of scuffled resistance preceded a response.

"I'm in no mood to play nice." Eddie recognized the voice as Jim's. "We can do this the hospitable way in the comfort of your fortress, or I can escort you to my drafty station house where the coffee is bad and the chairs are worse."

"Can you give me a minute?"

"Absolutely. The last thing I want to see right now is too much of you."

"Give the phone back to Bruce." The low muffle buzzed again.

"I'm so sorry about that, Mr. Emerson," the security chief apologized.

"No worries. Just keep them there. I'll call you right back."

"Very good, sir."

Eddie walked back to the great room where Kelly, Tori, and Lucas had settled. Flames from the dual-sided natural gas fireplace in the room's center warmed the air and ambiance of the surroundings. "Jim and Paul are downstairs," Eddie announced.

"What a surprise." Cecily set a tray of silver-base-and-handled glass cappuccino cups and a carafe on the oval glass and brass coffee table in front of the U-shaped sectional. "Not so much. I expected they'd show up."

"Why?" Kelly poured and filled the cups. "They weren't there last night. What went down shouldn't be their problem."

"No. But by association, we are," Cecily said.

"If I don't let Jim up here, he'll get a warrant," Eddie said.

"You don't have to say anything, Lucas," Kelly said.

"That's right," Cecily confirmed. "You can claim diplomatic immunity. I'm a lawyer. I'll say I'm representing Tori and ..."

"No." Lucas shook his head. "This has gone too far for long enough." He looked at Eddie. "I will talk to them."

"You're the boss." Eddie walked back to the phone and called Bruce. He crossed the floor and waited for the elevator doors to open.

Jim looked Eddie up and down. "You're dressed. Is Kelly decent?"

"Always, and we're not alone." Eddie led the detectives into his home.

Jim strolled past Eddie, glanced around at the group, and rubbed his hands together. "Well, how convenient. We're all here. The diplomat and his lady friend. Even my old partner. Morning, Cecily. Have you met Paul Callaway?"

Cecily frowned at Jim and smiled at Paul. "We've met in court."

Lucas stood. "We have not. Lucas Dominguez." He stuck out his hand. Paul shook it. "My fiancée Victoria."

"Fiancée?" Kelly's eyebrows lifted with the question in her voice.

"Congratulations, girlfriend!" Cecily sat beside Tori and patted her knee. "When did this happen?"

"Monday night, the day after the break-in." Tori snuggled up to Lucas. "We haven't told anyone else yet. You're the first."

"Well, it's a bit early in the day for champagne," Kelly said.

"We don't keep it around anyway," Eddie said. "But we do have sparkling water."

"Hell-OH." Jim took off his coat and tossed it on the back of the nearest unoccupied bit of sectional couch. "I hate to break up this impromptu celebration, but we're here on official business. And we've got a lot of ground to cover."

"Ask your questions, detective." Lucas held Tori's hand in both of his. "I will tell you what I can."

"OK, let's start simple." Jim sat on the cushion and his coat. Paul stood next to his partner, the notebook and pen from his pocket in hand. "Why, with all the firepower of the Canadian government in your bunker, did you hire a couple of local PIs?"

Victoria spoke up. "I actually hired them."

"Yeah, I know that," Jim said. "My good buddy Eddie didn't provide names or details when he asked my advice on how to find a missing person who might not want to be found." He turned to Lucas. "That, I presume, was you. And here you are. So, who is it you want them to find?"

Lucas breathed in and let it out slowly. His dark-eyed gaze leveled with Jim's. "The daughter of the woman I loved and lost." Lucas summed up the purpose for and the events that led up to and including his unexplained disappearance.

"Who was the guy in Buenos Aires that told you to keep the cops out of it and get out?" Jim asked.

"I have no idea," Lucas answered. "I asked at the front desk when I checked out of the hotel. No one there had seen him before."

"Huh." Jim rubbed his chin. "Did the consulate know where you were and why you went?"

"They knew I was in Argentina on personal business. Nothing more."

"What have you told them since you got back?"

"The subject didn't come up again until the boy delivered the mate cup."

Paul stopped taking notes. "What boy?" he asked.

"A Latino boy brought a cloth bag with the cup that had belonged to the Ruiz family to the consulate. He said it was for me in Quebec."

"He didn't know you were in Chicago," Paul said.

"No, I don't think so."

"What did this boy look like?" Paul asked.

"I was not there at the time. I was told he was maybe twelve or thirteen years of age. He spoke Spanish. He was poorly dressed but very polite."

Paul and Jim exchanged looks. "So, you think the cup came from this missing daughter?"

Lucas nodded. "Rayen. Or her mother. It is the only possible explanation."

Jim's attention shifted to Eddie and Cecily. "How and why did you two end up at Rush Memorial ER last night?"

"That is also on me, detective," Lucas said. "I asked them to take a letter to Rayen."

Jim scratched the balding spot above his forehead. "I'm confused. You knew where she was?"

Kelly jumped in. "I snapped a photo of her when Eddie and I were staking out the bodega. Then I tracked the laptop stolen from Lucas's apartment to a location near the bodega where we think Rayen wired the money."

"You can do that?" Jim asked.

"It's called lo-jacking," Paul explained. "The department uses it to locate stolen cars and equipment."

"I'll be damned," Jim said. "As old as I am, I still learn something new every day. So," he looked from Eddie to his former partner, "walk and talk me through this. Every move. All of it." He listened while Paul's pen filled pages in his notebook.

Jim sat back and slapped his palms on his knees as the testimony wound down. "I gotta tell you, folks, I'm not liking what I'm hearing. It's the writing on the apartment door. So far, you've all gotten off easy."

"Easy!" Eddie huffed. "We were shot at! They returned for a second strafing run after I ran Cecily's car over a curb."

"Jim's right, Eddie," Cecily said. "They plugged the back fender. An intentional miss."

"Point taken," Paul agreed. "The soldiers in this turf war shoot to kill, and the laptop added to their stockpile of ammunition."

Lucas looked from Jim to Paul, his anxiety apparent with his expression's elevated level of confusion and pain. "I don't understand."

"The laptop was an easy grab," Cecily said. "The message on the door was a warning to back off. They want to know why you were in Buenos Aires, what you were sent to find out, and who talked to you," Cecily said.

"But no one would tell me anything!" Lucas said.

"They don't know that," Cecily replied. "And we don't know the link between you, the laptop, and what could be on it that they'd want."

"Your laptop is protected by a passcode, correct?" Paul asked Lucas.

"Yes, of course."

"Are you the only staff person at the Chicago consulate who knows that code?" asked Paul.

Lucas closed his eyes and swallowed hard. "The consulate general can retrieve it from Ottawa if necessary. But he doesn't know it. Only I do."

Eddie exhaled and groaned an audible "Oh. I see where we're going with this, and I don't like it either. If they've found out about the money order and who sent it."

"They'll use Rayen as the bait," Cecily said.

"That lures Lucas into a trap," Kelly added.
"To get the passcode any way they can," Eddie concluded.

Chapter 29

The Letter

The bag in the hand of the stranger on her knees outside the alley window confirmed what Rayen knew in her heart to be true. The man her mother sent her away to find had found her.

Excitement overrode habitual caution. Rayen ran to the door and plowed all the force her shoulder could withstand against the heavy metal. Rusted hinges clunked and creaked on the third agonizing try. A child of the street in a tattered red coat with no buttons handed Rayen the bag and ran.

"Chica!" she called out. She panicked at the sounds of stomps and shouts from overhead. *The Bastardo's men!* Rayen escaped to the place where she'd hidden what she'd saved to help her leave this hell. She coaxed the loose brick from crumbling mortar and stashed her now most prized possession within the wall.

Dusk dissolved to the artificial lights of urban black and blue night. Rayen crouched on the mattress in her prison with the splintered door. She hugged her knees. Listened for the Bastardo's return. Braced for a beating. Let the memories of her mother play out behind closed eyes, and the hope for a future with Lucas Dominguez fill her with the prospect of joy. She dozed in snippets of ugly dreamed images. Working the streets in Buenos Aires for a handful of pesos, her mother could hide from that other bastardo who was not her father.

Counting the dollars Otto demanded from girls in the sex trade, boys in begging rings, and men taking livelihoods and lives in the kill-or-be-killed world ruled by her warden.

She waited for the apricot sliver of daylight bent through the window's filth in swirling dust. In the silence, she moved like a cat, on paws with claws retracted to the hiding place that concealed the bag. Carefully she inched the brick toward her without a speck of mortar falling. She stood with the bag in the light and peered inside at the letter-sized envelope with her name written on it. Her hands trembled. Her fingers fumbled. She unfolded and smoothed the creased paper.

Strong ink strokes of flowing cursive filled the page, the words written in both the Spanish and English of their shared native land.

> My Dearest Rayen,
>
> I am as desperate to find you as you are to find me. Luck or fate has intervened on our behalf. We are both in Chicago.
> Men who are determined to keep us apart have stolen a laptop computer with information vital to the national security of Canada and the safety of others living beyond my country's borders. This information can only be accessed by a passcode assigned to me. The laptop's location can be tracked when the device is activated.
> This laptop is in the building where you are. Find it. Turn it on so that I may find you.
> I must return to Canada soon. I made a promise to your grandmother at her grave that I will not leave without you. Your mother is no longer in Buenos Aires. I regret that I don't know where she is. We will find her together.
> I promise you. Your new life is about to begin.
>
> All my love,
> Lucas

She read and reread the message. Imagined hearing his voice speak the words in both languages. She hugged the letter to her chest and felt her heart beat in tandem with his. "Te quiero, papa," she whispered. For the first time in a long while, Rayen smiled through her tears.

"Here, I make the rules." Otto's dismissal of a warning against killing a foreign diplomat abruptly wrenched Rayen's relief to fear. "No, Papa!" she whispered. "You must not come here for me! I will find this laptop and bring it to you!"

Chapter 30

The Dragon

Otto hungered for power as an infant's lips grope for its mother's nipple. He didn't crave it as an addict or an alcoholic dependent on the next fix or flow from a bottle. Those weaknesses could be controlled through medical intervention, counseling, or peer support. Power was the daily bread that filled his belly and nourished the blood in his veins. His need for more was insatiable. Its loss or access to it would kill him.

The stolen laptop object of his obsession lay closed and coiled like a silent serpent. The lid opened to a flat screen of blackness. The round button entry to power taunted him. *Push it, and the serpent hisses its signal. Push it, and you're mine, boludo!*

Acquiring and selling firearms, from the smallest semi-automatic pistol to the deadliest assault rifle, bankrolled and fortified his operations and ambitions for expansion. Otto fired a weapon only when necessary. Street soldiers that protected all he claimed and conquered carried out his shoot-to-kill orders. Otto stoked his flame with up-close-and-personal physical force and blood on a sharp blade.

He closed his eyes and envisioned a soldier's gun barrel buried at the base of the laptop owner's brain. The serpent's passcode coaxed from his lips. The knife in Otto's hands. A scream silenced by the blade.

The crunch of a fist striking jaw snapped Otto back into the moment. "That slice and dice was my hit!" The gangbanger Otto had tag-named Scruggs for his stumpy stature and disgusting eating habits stood over the punk he'd punished. "The dead kid was yours. Don't ever dump your shit on my turf!" Scruggs hauled his half-conscious conquest up and onto wobbly feet. He shook the skin-over-bones-thin man like a rag doll. "I can't even take a piss in an alley without the cops up my ass!"

"Fuck that!" Spit flew with the angry snarl from another of Otto's lieutenants. The tall one that always wore a suit but never a tie slapped a flat palm on Otto's desk. "Where's my shipment of pocket pistols? And the kilos from Colombia Vasquez promised?"

"Vasquez promised us some fresh Latina skin months ago!" a banger without a name complained.

"Shut the fuck up!" Otto bellowed. "I always get you what you need! Now get out and make me rich! Dragon!" Otto summoned the warrior he knew only by the ink in his arm. He halted halfway to the door.

"That's not my name." Dragon turned deliberate and slowly toward the powder keg of a boss with a perpetually lit fuse.

Otto's curled lip uncovered the space where a canine tooth once was. "I don't give a fuck what your name is. Where's the stuttering gimp?"

"Watching Rayen as you told him to. Making sure she doesn't go anywhere. Following her if she does."

No one had ever intimidated Otto. The quiver of doubt that rippled through him under this man's hard, emotionless stare surprised then angered Otto. He fought off and dispersed a feeling unnatural and unknown. "What did that chica give the street kid to hand over to Vasquez's bitch daughter?"

Every muscle in Dragon's body stiffened. He'd fired the shot at the banged-up Chevy and missed the reason for the chase. Dragon seethed behind the frozen mask of indifference. He had been one-upped by a woman and a fool. "I don't know what you're talking about."

"You don't know." Otto wagged his head from side to side. "What I don't know makes me crazy. Here's what I don't know. Vasquez has dropped out of sight and off the grid. He's not delivered what he regularly supplies. I need to know why." He leaned with his hip against the desk and folded his arms over his chest. "Maybe Rayen knows. Maybe that's what the chica in the alley handed off to the street kid." His quiet smirk spread to a full body language shout. Otto stabbed a shaky crooked finger at the laptop. "Maybe the answers

118

are here. It makes me crazy that I can't get to them." The crooked finger pointed at his desk chair. "I want the man who does to sit in that chair. That is what I told you and the stuttering gimp to make happen."

Shoulders shrugged under a denim jacket. "I'm working on it."

Otto's remaining teeth clenched with his fists. The hammer of flesh struck wood. The laptop bounced in protest. "No more! Now I tell you what I will do." Otto opened the laptop and pointed at the power button. "I will turn this on. Then I will call that diplomat at the embassy and tell him to come and get it."

Dragon lunged at the laptop and slammed the lid closed. "Do that, and you'll get nothing. Think!" He tapped a finger from the arm with the tattoo to his temple. "You've already said it. Why did the chica in the alley take such a risk? What did she deliver? What connection does the daughter of your South American supplier of drugs, weapons, and women for the sex trade have to a Canadian diplomat?"

Rage pounding in Otto's ears cleared as Dragon talked. He heard. He saw. Rayen trussed like an animal about to be slaughtered, telling him all he wanted to know as the serpent uncoils and the tortured diplomat dies.

Otto glared at the man he'd tagged Dragon. "A shipment will be here in three days. You have three days to deliver that diplomat to me."

Chapter 31

The Raid

As raids go, this one should have been routine. The anonymous tip was relayed from Sergeant Decker Melrose's South Side station house to Sergeant Brenda Talbot's office less than an hour after the ME's report landed on Jim's desk. The DNA from body parts in the dumpster near where the boy's remains were found matched the hand in the Argentine restaurant's trash that had once belonged to Carlos Delgado.

The detective's CO stopped mid-stride between their workstations long enough to secure the bulletproof vest over her department issue winter jacket. "Grab your gear, gentlemen," Sergeant Talbot ordered. "All available hands on deck, 3400 block Cermak Road."

Paul suited up and holstered his Glock. "Isn't that about where Eddie crashed Cecily's car and almost met his maker?"

"Damn near." Jim beat his partner to the set of keys and followed the line of plainclothes and uniforms to the official fleet of parked unmarked cars and squads.

The brigade of flashing lights and siren blasts cut to dark and silent on command a half mile away from the empty industrial space for sale or lease. Vehicles surrounded the single-floor flat roof structure marked by amateur artist attempts at murals and gang symbols. A mini-army of urban soldiers got into position behind the cover of cars, head-to-knee body shields, and any solid protection. An elderly woman in the sheltered bus stop at the curb by a barred and padlocked side door clutched the handles of a big box store shopping bag. An officer approached and helped her swiftly and safely away from the scene.

"Clear." Radios on all sides of the eight thousand square foot cement block building signaled go. Officers commanded by Sergeant Melrose took the lead entry point position at the vulnerable rear drive-in bays. A stripped-down panel van without tires or doors and no engine under the missing hood withered in its rust at the weed-pocked edge of the property.

Paul crouched beside his partner alongside their unmarked car. "If anyone is inside, they came on foot," he observed.

Jim glanced up and around. His eyes focused on tire tread marks in the cold mist-dampened dust. "Or they drove through and closed the doors." He keyed his radio and asked a general question. "Ross. Any activity?"

"No apparent movement." Lead officer reports trailed in over police frequency. "The windows are covered." "All the doors are locked from the outside." "The bay doors aren't." "Voices heard." "How many?" "Hard to tell."

Sudden straight-line light under and between the bay doors sliced the mid-afternoon gloom. "Engines!" Jim registered the radioed alert seconds before the bay doors opened.

"Police!" The warning shouts and guns drawn didn't deter the drivers or their armed passengers. Chicago's finest scrambled to avoid being hit by bumpers and bullets.

"Fuck, I hate it when I'm right." Jim braced his firing arm on the hood of the car and shot out the windshield of the sedan barreling toward him and his partner's position. The thud of impact rocked the vehicle that, remarkably, remained on all four tires.

"Cover me!" Paul shouted.

"Where the hell are you going!" Jim skimmed against the passenger's side doors toward the back of the car and repeated his stance over the trunk. Paul had hooked his forearms under the armpits of a uniformed officer, prone and bleeding into the concrete cracks and faded lines of parking slot paint. Their bodies rolled in side-to-side opposition. Jim cursed under his breath as Paul dragged living dead weight.

"Officers down!" Melrose radioed dispatch. "Buses and backup at Cermak Road location!"

Jim's attention darted from the scene before him to the situation at his feet. Able officers protected by shields crossed the warehouse threshold and emptied vehicles of ambulatory occupants at gunpoint. The injured lay, sat, or limped on the inner-city battlefield. Paul's fingers pressed on the femoral artery bleed from the downed officer's left thigh.

Sergeant Talbot reached in the window of the car t-boned into the vehicle that shielded Jim and Paul. "Ross? Callaway?" she called out.

"Present and accounted for," Jim replied.

The sergeant moved in the direction of her detective's voice. "You OK?"

Jim holstered his sidearm. "We are, but he isn't."

"Neither is the driver of that car," she said. "You took the shot?"

"Afraid so," Jim said. "How bad?"

"Alive. Uncertain." She knelt beside Paul and the officer he'd saved. "I'll take over." Her press slowed the bleeding more. "Check in with Sergeant Collier. Get medics over here when the scene is secure."

The detectives stepped out into controlled pandemonium. Medic units with gurneys and defibrillators arrived with law enforcement brandishing weapons and handcuffs. The triage and prisoner roundup continued while the gray day aged to dusk. Jim and Paul aided in the warehouse search for suspect stragglers and illegal contraband. After hours of no evidence collected, the operation was called off. But the interrogation was on.

***

Complaints ricocheted in waves of profanity off the walls of the South Side station house lockup. The loudest chords of discontent jangled from and between the lieutenants of rival managers in illegal trade.

"I swear on your butt-ugly mother's grave, I will cut you up and use you for rat bait!" Thin lips pulled taut over jagged teeth spewed threats across the abyss to the opposite cell. The white-knuckle clench of fists on the bars rattled the locked door.

"You'll be a corpse before you pick up the knife!" his adversary fired back.

"Civility, please!" Sergeant Melrose paced the cement between cells. Sergeant Talbot stood at military attention, keen to observe and question should the course require correction.

"There's nothing civilized about that hijo de puta." Muscles in the shorter man's stumpy arms twitched. He jabbed shaky fingers at his chest and in the air for angry emphasis. "We came to get what was ours. He'd already stolen all of it!"

The red face behind the other cell bars contorted from above, simmering to boiling rage. "You lying sack of shit! There was nothing there to take!"

Melrose held his hands up with palms out in a traffic cop stop signal directed at each of the incarcerated. "Hold on! What were you there to divvy up?"

Silence descended.

"Alright, we'll get back to that." Melrose crossed and stood toe-to-toe on the other side of the bars with the gang banger he knew. "C'mon, Scruggy. Use what you've got left between your ears. How did we know you were there if we weren't tipped off?"

Scruggy moved to his left, sucked in whatever clogged his nostrils and spit the contents past the man in uniform. "Ask him."

His rival returned the bodily function insult. "The rat came out of your sewer!"

"Enough!" The sergeant's booming baritone echoed off and around the concrete chamber. His hard stare shifted between the arrested. "It's obvious neither of you is capable of pulling anything close to cleared heads out of your asses. So, I guess that unpleasant task falls on our shoulders." Melrose glanced at Sergeant Talbot, turned, and paced the length of the center aisle between cells. "I get a call from an informant who won't leave his name or tell me where he's calling from. He gives me an address and a time when you and your pals will all be together under that same roof conducting business that damn sure ain't legal. So, we show up. And there you are. But the building is empty. Nothing of real value. Only the junk that previous tenants and the homeless left behind." Melrose stopped, shoved his hands in his pants pockets, and stared at the floor. "This makes me wonder why we were all invited to this party. You didn't get what you came for. I've got injured officers and a full lockup of gang bangers to process, prosecute and put away. So, tell me." Melrose glared at his prisoners. "Who won?"

The lid on Scruggy's simmer spouted. He roared his rage in a rapid-fire tirade of slang-peppered Spanish broken only by names and an insult identifiable in almost any language.

123

Sergeant Talbot motioned a request for silence between them that Melrose understood, then signaled him to follow her out of the cell block and away from the sputter of residual steam from Otto's incoherent lieutenant.

"I couldn't understand a word of that gibberish," Melrose said. "Did you?"

"Yes. All of it." She walked ahead and toward his office. "I want Detectives Ross and Callaway in on this."

Chapter 32

Funeral Flowers

Shadows embraced Otto's Dragon like the prodigal son returned. He'd abandoned that protection when survival no longer required hiding in the crevices and curves of darkness. A childhood that wasn't had chewed him up and spit him out onto the streets. Doorways sheltered him. Stray dogs huddled around him in dark patches shared for warmth. Shadows concealed him as he stalked marked prey with wallets in back pockets and purses easily opened. He hadn't dodged the light since he'd choked the life from the frightened boy within. The fear was gone. But the self-taught skill that had kept him alive returned on command.

Dragon tailed his prey in the human blind of December city congestion made denser by suburban dwellers and tourists toting shopping bags and luggage on rollers. The hatless man with a lion's mane of black hair streaked silver wearing a charcoal gray wool topcoat over predictable blue or black suits made tracking his movements easier. Dragon could set the watch he didn't have on his quarry's habitual punctuality. He'd cross the main entrance into One Prudential Plaza precisely at seven thirty-five every weekday morning. Emerge twelve minutes later with a large to go coffee. Push through the glass revolving doors of Two Pru Plaza at seven fifty-two. Leave the building at ten minutes past five. At the end of a brisk walk through Millennium Park, he'd trod steps guarded by bronze lions into the arms of a lover named Victoria.

Dragon had battled hours of boredom under the veneer of feigned interest in American Art after 1940. Spied the bounce of loose ginger curls on squared shoulders. Got close enough for a sideways glance to read the nametag on the suit jacket lapel over her right breast. Noticed the name of the florist that delivered a bouquet of lilies to the front desk. Saw delight in her green eyes as she buried her nose in the blooms.

His plan to lure the diplomat, as Otto had commanded, required a double simultaneous punch. Dragon visited the florist. He ordered white lilies to be delivered to the Art Institute. Using an untraceable burner phone, he called the Canadian Consulate and left a voicemail message for Lucas Dominguez.

***

Tori closed the conference room door on the last meeting in a long day of them. "Great job." The echoed quick clack of her low pump heels down the hard surface hallway muffled the mumble. "But we need you to raise twenty percent more." She nudged her hip against the last door on the right, stepped into her private workspace, and closed the door. *"And just how am I supposed to work that miracle?"*

The scent of lilies nestled in a vase on her desk shifted frustration with the board and her boss to the joyful anticipation of a future near and far away. "Mon amour." She crossed the room and caressed the fragile petals devoid of the usual burst of color Lucas always sent. "That's odd. It's Christmastime, not Easter." Tori tugged the card from the envelope and dropped it. The somber greeting without a name flickered like a flame at her fingertips, turning her stomach to ice.

***

Lucas mentally checked off this day's end to-do list. Emails sent. Calls returned. He powered down his computer and played back the last voicemail message.

"You want Rayen. Passcode required. Ask your chula about the flowers."

The receiver fell from his hand to the desk. Anger jangled every nerve. Fear unleashed the wild within. He called the top contact on his cell phone. Swore oaths in every language he knew in the anxious wait for Tori's answer. "Were flowers delivered to you today?" he asked her.

"Yes. From the florist you always use. They came with a sympathy card."

His free fist clenched. The hand that held the phone shook. "Was there a name on the card?"

"No. Only mine on the envelope and delivery order. I thought you sent them. But I knew you hadn't when I saw what was inside. Lucas." The tremble in her voice blew him apart. "White lilies are for funerals."

"Victoria, listen to me. Call security. Stay in your office. Lock the door."

"What are you going to do?"

"I'm not sure yet."

"Lucas, please. Promise me you won't do something crazy."

He couldn't. "Promise me you won't leave the museum. Will you do that for me, love?" Seconds of connected silence stretched his taut nerves to the breaking point.

"Call me back in fifteen minutes." The controlled demand in her tone worried him. "I mean it, Lucas."

He glanced at his wristwatch. "I will." Lucas told Tori he loved her and called Eddie with his own demand. "I went along with your plan, and it failed. Rayen is still in danger, and now Victoria has been threatened. I can no longer sit by and do nothing. So, I'm asking you again. Will you help me, Eddie?"

Chapter 33

The Decoy

Ben Perez had aimed for this assignment with every bullet fired in practice at moving targets.

In college classrooms, through cadet training and seventeen years in uniform, he'd tasted the anticipated adrenaline rush of serving with an elite law enforcement team. The thrill of deep dive undercover with a name and identity suited to the role he was about to play. Proving to his CO and the city's top brass, he was ready for the gold shield step toward a commander's oak leaves.

The buzz and hum of pre-briefing tension circled the long rectangle of conference table and occupied chairs. Ben knew most of those chosen. Detective Jim Ross, a respected veteran and department legend, primed to retire. His partner, Detective Paul Callaway on a fast track to command. Maybe as high as top cop. Uniforms and detectives any officer on the force would trust with his or her back. Foreign agents identified by RCMP patches and CSIS royal blue huddled together at the far end of the table, their faces stern and voices low.

Ben ran his finger under the collar of the white business shirt chafing the skin on his neck. He tugged at the cuffs on the black suit jacket and picked at the perfect crease in the pants. *Not exactly gang rags,* Ben thought. *I wonder who the hell I'm supposed to be.*

Sergeant Decker Melrose followed Sergeant Brenda Talbot into the room. The commanding officers from separate station houses stood at the head of the table. Sergeant Bill Collier, a former detective promoted the day Jim Ross got his gold shield, was already seated at the table.

Sergeant Talbot opened the briefing.

"Corroborated information from reliable sources confirms the location of suspects in the dismemberment murders and theft of a laptop that is the property of the Canadian government. A member of the South Side human trafficking operation arrested and incarcerated after yesterday's raid of the vacant warehouse on Cermak Road identified Otto Hermann as the boss that ordered the hits, and he is apparently in possession of the laptop."

"Sarge, was Hermann the source of the guns and drugs tip on an empty building?" asked a detective Ben knew from the narcotics unit.

"According to our prisoner, there is a high probability Hermann took advantage of an opportunity to put his rivals in our lockup and profit from all contraband delivered by a dealer in South America," Sergeant Talbot replied. "Source says a shipment is due in three days."

"Do we know the name of the dealer?" a uniformed officer asked.

"Luis Vasquez," Sergeant Melrose said. "Runs guns, drugs, and women for the sex trade out of Buenos Aires. He recently expanded into Colombia and Venezuela when the government and authorities in Argentina started cracking down on his business."

"Vasquez," Ben overheard Callaway ask Ross. "Isn't that the same last name of the woman Eddie and Kelly were hired to find?"

"By God, you're right," Ross replied, "it is."

"It could be a fairly common name," Callaway said, "or just a coincidence."

"Could be," Ross said, "but that's too much of a coincidence to be one."

Callaway snorted. "And you don't believe in coincidences."

"Got that right," Ross agreed.

"So where does the laptop fit in with the murders and contraband?" asked an officer with the letters ATF in all caps across his bulletproof vest.

"The murders were intended to start a turf war for Hermann to expand and sell the excess contraband inventory for a bigger profit," Sergeant Talbot said.

The CSIS agent swiveled in her chair and made eye contact with everyone around the table. "A diplomat from the Canadian Consulate was looking into the case file of a mother and daughter with the Vasquez family name. The laptop was stolen from our diplomat's apartment after he returned from Buenos Aires."

Ross leaned back in his chair and looked at the ceiling tiles stained by an old or perhaps new roof leak. "While this is all very entertaining, do we have a plan?"

"Recovery of the laptop is the top priority of our Canadian counterparts." Sergeant Talbot gestured to the RCMP officer. "Inspector Freeland can speak to that."

"Thank you." The inspector leaned forward on his elbows and folded his hands on the table. "The Consulate General requested the laptop passcode from Ottawa. That passcode will temporarily activate the device so that we can pinpoint its exact location. Agent Cartier and I will move in and secure the laptop when all team members are in position. We will in no way impede or assist in your arrest and apprehension efforts."

Ross sat up straight and focused on the inspector. "What about Rayen Vasquez? Are you going to get her out?"

The Canadian officers exchanged glances. "How do you know that name?" Agent Cartier asked.

Ross pointed to the badge on his vest. "I'm still in charge of that breaking and entering case when the laptop was stolen from your diplomat's apartment. The name came up in conversations my partner and I had with Lucas Dominguez."

Agent Cartier's gaze locked on Ross. "Immigration has reopened the Vasquez case file. That is all I am prepared to reveal at this time."

"Huh. That so?" Ross rubbed at the stubble on his chin and glanced at Ben. "So why is Perez dressed up like he's got a hot date at the yacht club?"

Sergeant Talbot cut off the awkward exchange with an explanation. "Officer Perez's undercover assignment and identity as Lucas Dominguez will create the diversion needed to apprehend Otto Hermann," she said.

"You mean he's the decoy to draw Hermann out in the open." Ross whistled through his teeth and clapped Ben on the shoulder. "I sure hope that gold shield or whatever it is you've been promised is worth it."

Ben started to sweat under the shirt's starched collar.

Chapter 34

Dragon's Surprise

A stifling net of suspicion tightened around Rayen. The distinctive stutter scrape step of Otto's tenacious watchdog followed her every move. Midnights and mornings, she heard his shuffle on the other side of the old new door to her prison. The locked replacement for what Otto had assaulted and splintered in a fit of rage. The watchdog held the key that let her out into a limited world of tending to daily necessities and paperwork tracking the ebb and flow of Otto's felonious acquisition of wealth.

The laptop never moved from the epicenter of Otto's desk. Rayen watched him guard his obsession from her corner of the room. Stalk the inanimate object. He circled like a shark blinded by a lack of acuity to comprehend the curious prize. Every plan to escape and return what belonged to her father to him dissolved with her nightly tears of frustration.

Rayen desperately needed a diversion. A call to action against a threat her warden could not ignore.

***

Eddie clutched keys to the Jeep in one hand and his cell phone in the other. "Lucas, I gotta tell you, man. I'm not liking where this is going."

"All I ask is that you look after Victoria for me. Please. Get her to safety. Give me the address where I can find Rayen. I'll go there alone."

Eddie winced at his client's reply. "I can't let you do that." Headlights flashed with the beep and unlock of the vehicle's door. "Stay where you are. I'm on my way. I want to hear this voicemail message. I'll call Kelly. We'll figure something else out." Eddie ended one call and called home. "Kel?" He buckled into the driver's seat and started the car. "I'm going to see Lucas at his office."

"Oh? Yet another meeting I'm not invited to."

"We don't have time for this. Listen, he's worried about Tori. Something about flowers delivered to the Art Institute and a sympathy card with no name. Take Petula. Go pick her up. Get her to the penthouse and turn on every security bell and whistle we've got."

"You're kidding me, right? You want me to drive Petula into the Loop at rush hour the week before Christmas?"

"Just do it, Kel. Call me when you get back home." Eddie steered the Jeep south into gridlock traffic on Lake Shore Drive. He tapped the brakes to avoid bending fenders with the slow-rolling Prius in front of him and flashed a warning to the driver behind the headlights in the rearview mirror.

Nearly forty minutes into a usual ten-minute drive, Eddie spotted Lucas waving from the curb in front of Two Pru Plaza. A taxi's horn honked at the Jeep's swerved intrusion. Lucas got in and buckled up. "I forwarded the message to my phone. Victoria?"

"Kelly is on the way to the museum. She'll be safe at our place."

Lucas exhaled in relief. His chin dropped to his chest. "Thank you." He played back the message on his cell phone.

Eddie's grip on the steering wheel turned his knuckles white. "We should go to the police with this."

Lucas stared through the windshield. His facial muscles flexed with the firm clamp of his jaw. "I must get to Rayen."

"C'mon, Lucas. Think about this. How are we going to do that? It's not like we can walk up and knock on the door. Cecily couldn't even hand over a note to Rayen. We were shot at trying to get away."

"They want the laptop passcode. I can give that to them. They will give her to me."

"No, they won't. We're dealing with hardcore career criminals here. We don't know if she got your message. Assuming she did, that she's still alive and where Cecily last saw her, as soon as you give them the passcode, both you and Rayen will be expendable. Of no further use. Do you understand what I'm saying?"

Lucas turned and looked at Eddie. "All too well." The hurt in his eyes and tone of his voice projected a lifetime of coping with the searing memory of pain and loss.

"Look, man, I'm..." The cell phone ring cut off his attempt to soften the blow. "Kel? You home?"

"Not yet." Her voice through the Jeep's incoming call system filled the car's interior. "We stopped at Tori's apartment to pick up Cassie."

"Lucas?" The tense mix of fear and anger in Victoria's voice came through loud and clear. "It's been way more than fifteen minutes."

"I know, mon amour," Lucas responded. "I'm sorry."

"Are you breaking another promise and dragging Eddie into some crazy danger with you?" Tori asked him. "Answer me!"

Lucas rubbed his forehead and traced the lines around closed eyes with the tips of his fingers. "Turn the car around," he said to Eddie.

"With pleasure." Eddie steered the Jeep onto a side street he recognized too late. Lit up squad cars with blaring sirens swarmed like angry hornets. Traffic parted to avoid being stung.

"Holy hell!" Eddie swerved and slammed on the brakes.

***

Everything about this best plan to bring down Otto Hermann felt wrong to Jim.

"What's wrong with it?" Paul adjusted the device in his ear. "In position," he responded from the front seats of an unmarked car parked to strategically block an alleyway escape attempt.

"I don't know exactly." Jim sat rigid and unbuckled behind the steering wheel. "I can't put my finger on it. All I know is this mutt won't just roll over. Every time he's been cornered, arrested, taken to court, or locked up, he's found a way to beat it and us. There's no way he doesn't have a plan B and a few more letters of the alphabet on his dance card as backup. Then there's this business about the passcode firing up the laptop. The Canucks were so keen on getting it back. Why wait until now?"

"I asked that question after the briefing and got a short answer from Sergeant Talbot," Paul said. "Coordination and cooperation."

Jim snorted. "Shorthand for so the hometown troops could fight their battle."

A gust of wind down the manmade tunnel between buildings lifted and flapped a heavy, faded camouflage green tarp that covered an oversized utility-grade metal frame on thick run-flat tires. Steel installed against brick rattled at the rear of Otto's two-story fortress anchored below ground to a walk-out basement accessed by a short stack of concrete steps.

"God, I hate it when the weatherman gets it right." Jim squinted into falling snow at the forty-five-degree angled and sloped half-moon metal slide from the rooftop to a shallow debris bin below. "That's no fire escape I've ever seen. What the hell is it?"

Paul glanced in the direction where Jim pointed. "Trash chute?"

"Could be. But why is it coming from the roof?"

"Flat roofs leak. These buildings are old."

"Possibly. But that looks too permanent for a one-off repair job." Movement in shadows where light rarely reached rippled in Jim's peripheral vision. "What the ..." Jim nudged Paul with his elbow. "Tell me you see that."

"See what?" Paul peered through the windshield. "I don't... wait a second." He squinted at the shadows. "I'm not sure. Whatever it is, I don't like it." Paul opened the passenger side door, dropped, and crouched on the concrete. "Cover me."

"Now what?" Jim yanked the keys from the ignition and the Glock from its holster. "Oh, for fuck's sake." He stifled a reactive groan when pain seized his bent knees.

Paul clung to the backs of buildings. His fingers traced straight brick mortar lines to crumbling corners. Rubber soles on his shoes followed smooth tracks, intermittent scraped lines left in mud, and the odd patch of dirty snow under a coating of fresh crystals. An elusive form took shape. The black jacket sleeve above the wrist of the hand that held the blade crept up the tattooed forearm. An inked red line tongue twitched with the flex of muscles around the chest of a man dressed in a black suit. The knife blade flashed on flesh exposed by an open dress shirt collar.

Dragon had taken the decoy prisoner.

"Perez has been marked," Paul reported in to the law enforcement team com link. "He's headed into the building. By force."

Jim flattened his back against the bricks beside Paul. "Shit! This plan stinks in places even I didn't smell." He glanced around their surroundings. "Got any ideas?" he asked his partner.

"I thought you would." Paul cupped his palm around his ear and frowned. "They sure as hell don't."

Orders crackled through the detectives' earpieces. "Proceed as planned. Block stairways and exits. Secure and arrest all suspects."

Jim groaned. "So that's their answer. Send in the stormtroopers." He shook his head and hissed out a protest. "You have got to be kidding me."

Paul drew his weapon and prepared for battle. "I guess Perez is expendable."

"Copy that," Jim agreed, "and apparently, so is Rayen."

***

Otto paced within arm's length of the stolen gift he couldn't open.

Damn Vasquez! He cursed the man responsible for his escalating agitation. Where are the guns? The drugs? The women! He glared at the daughter of the supplier, who hadn't delivered. Every scratch of Rayen's pencil on ledger sheets annoyed him. He resisted the urge to kill her and reminded himself why he needed her alive.

Dragon's deadline for delivery of the Canadian with the passcode that would spill the virtual guts of data from the device on his desk was up in less than six hours. "Where is that boludo?" Otto snarled at the laptop, and air choked a neck not yet there.

The sound of shoes scraping the hallway floor redirected Otto's pent-up wrath to the open doorway. The limp body of a well-dressed Latino flopped face down at his feet. Blood from an unseen wound spattered Otto's shoes.

"You fucking idiot!" he screamed at Dragon. "I told you to bring him to me. I get what I want, then I kill him!"

Dragon patted the folds of the black suit his victim wore. Perez moaned with the rough extraction of com link wire and a firearm from his possession.

Rayen cowered in the corner. *Papa! No!* She hugged herself to control the tremble and bit her lip to stifle the scream.

"He's not dead." Dragon tossed the earpiece and gripped the gun in his fist. "And he's not that diplomat. I know! I followed Dominguez for three days." The toe of Dragon's boot savagely connected with the downed officer's ribs. "He's a cop!"

Otto's face flushed as red as the bloodshot in his blue eyes." Why the fuck did you drop a cop at my feet! Where is that bastard with the passcode?"

Dragon blocked Otto's incoming fist, aimed for an uppercut to the chin, and punched the wind out of his angry attacker. He backed away but held his ground. Fists balled and ready to fight. "Don't you get it? The cops were using him to get to you and take us down!"

Otto gulped in breaths lost and glared at Dragon. "They try, they die," he panted.

The unmistakable sounds of assault and defense grew more intense. Urgent shouts. Shots fired. A small army marched in from the street.

"I'm telling you; we have got to get out now!" Dragon shouted.

Relief at the truth revealed had released Rayen's agony. Otto's anger fueled her strength. Shouts from the floor below emboldened her. She waited for her last and best chance to escape.

Leave me bastardo! Let me go! With his back to her and self-preserving focus aimed at unwitting the advancing invaders, she crawled across the room's pocked wood floor to the desk planted dead center between four walls. She reached for and snared his prize. Hugged it to her chest. The computer he coveted was hers now. Rayen folded her legs to kneel and hide from her tormenter. Waited. Prayed for a way out and on to the life her mother had sent her away to live and the man she'd promised would save her.

Soon, Papa. I will find you.

Rayen felt the device vibrate. The dormant computer had been remotely revived.

"I'm not going without that laptop!" Otto lurched past the prone body of Perez and staggered to his desk. Every muscle in his face contorted in ugly rage. He pounded his fists on the empty surface. "Where the fuck is it!"

The desk tilted as a leg buckled with the force of Otto's mighty kick. Rayen scrambled from her hiding place. She screamed at the ferocity of Otto's bruising vice grip on her arms above the elbows.

"You bitch whore thief!" Otto ripped the laptop away and pushed her into Dragon. "Fucking cops! I can play the baiting game, too. Bring her!" he ordered and headed for the stairs.

Chapter 35

The Chute

Players in the high-stakes game of law versus disorder clashed in a heated volley of verbal commands through com links, warning shouts, and the pop of gunfire.

Weapons ready, Jim and Paul headed back to the alley. The unmarked car they'd abandoned had lost headlights and the driver's side window to the crossfire of collateral damage.

"There's no position to hold, so screw plan A," Jim said. "Whaddya say we join the party? Go in through that basement door."

"Works for me," Paul replied. "Lead on."

Deserters that could run fled into the urban warren of residential side streets. Jim signaled the alley all clear. The detectives rounded the corner and crouched in the cement block stairwell.

Jim tried and cursed the locked and rusted door knob.

Paul picked at the frame with his fingernails. "Termites. This should be easy."

Jim groaned. "Nothing is that easy."

"Oh, ye of little faith," Paul said. "On three." The wood frame surrounding the lock splintered on the second battering try.

Semi-darkness and dampness, heavy with the earthy smell of mold, lay on the other side of the broken door. Jim and Paul proceeded cautiously down the dim hallway toward the stairs and the sounds of armed confrontation overhead.

"Ross. Callaway." Sergeant Talbot's voice crackled over their earpieces. "Suspects are on the run. Securing the building perimeter is priority one."

"The unmarked was shot up. We're in the building, Sarge," Jim responded.

"Location," she demanded.

"On the ground-level stairs up to the main floor," Jim confirmed.

"The Canadian officers need assistance getting to the second floor. Make that happen, detective."

"Copy that." Jim nodded to his partner. "Ready?"

"Set and go." Paul kicked open the door. Bullets fired from a semi-automatic weapon riddled the wood. The door hung loose on hinges with fewer screws. The partners regrouped in defensive shoulder-to-shoulder positions, their backs pressed to the wall.

Jim expelled breath held. "Pretty sure that wasn't friendly fire."

"Any chance for backup?"

Jim shook his head. "I got the feeling from Sarge we're it down here."

Paul glanced from Jim to the doorway. "I'll go right. You take left."

"I've got a better idea." Jim keyed his com link. "Freeland and Cartier. This is Ross."

"Go ahead, detective." Agent Cartier's clipped response rang clear through Jim's earpiece.

"Are either of you armed?"

"Both of us are," Inspector Freeland replied.

Jim looked for and spotted the opening to stairs and the second floor. "My partner and I are pinned down in the first-floor hallway about ten feet from the only way any of us are going to get upstairs to Hermann and that laptop."

"On our way," the CSIS agent said.

Paul snorted. "What the hell are they gonna do?"

Gunshots, the shuffle of feet, and cries of surprise from Otto's men echoed in the stairwell chamber.

"That," Jim said. "I'll take the left."

"Right." Paul bent his knees and sidestepped out of hiding. The lone man still standing took aim. Jim rolled to his left and fired. The wounded runaways lay on the floor, cursing their pain and defeat. Paul kicked away their weapons and wrestled the loudest protester into handcuffs.

Agent Cartier stepped over the downed. "Let's go," she said, heading for the stairs with Inspector Freeland on her heels.

"Sure. Leave the dirty work to us," Jim grumbled and handcuffed the wounded man who could have killed Callaway. He trailed Paul up the stairs as fast as his veteran legs could.

The scene at the top of the stairs mirrored what they'd left behind. Gang bangers who hadn't hit the exits soon enough were scattered on the floor or propped up against the wall, subdued by injuries minor to severe with metal bracelets around their wrists. A team of medics tended to a battered and unconscious Officer Perez.

Jim sized up the stern expressions and terse orders for backup delivered by the commanding officers tearing Otto's office apart and frowned. "I get the feeling this didn't go down so well." The tight-lipped lines of apparent frustration on the faces of the Canadians confirmed his suspicions. "What happened, Sarge?" Jim asked his CO. He glanced back at the human heaps in the hallway. "Where's Hermann?"

"Gone," was her one-word reply.

"What about Rayen?" Jim gestured toward Cartier and Freeland. "The woman their diplomat was looking for?"

"Still searching," Sergeant Talbot replied, "but so far, no women have been spotted on the premises."

"Hermann may have taken her with him and the laptop," Jim said.

"A hostage for insurance," Paul added.

Their CO nodded in agreement. "Possibly."

"That explains why our northern neighbors are so pissed off," Paul said. "Are we sure he was here?"

"The laptop is here in this building." Agent Cartier stepped up and interrupted the detectives' banter. Inspector Freeland approached and stood within arm's length of her. "The Consulate General accessed it remotely," he said. "It was confirmed the signal came from this location."

"Then where is it?" Jim rubbed his chin. "And where is Hermann?" He looked back at the stairway and steps leading up, snapped his fingers, and poked Paul's arm. "That trash chute."

Paul's eyes went wide. "The monster truck under the tarp."

"The roof!" they said together.

140

"C'mon!" Jim's legs churned with energy not seen or felt in years. He led the charge up the stairs and through a metal fire door open to the mid-December cold and blowing snow. The foursome ran across the flat surface toward the roar of an engine igniting below. Wide tires screeched on gripped cement. Metal crunched in ramming speed acceleration. The unmarked car Jim and Paul had abandoned fractured on impact. Law officers from both sides of the border watched as the reasons for risking their lives in the line of duty sped away in a modified Hummer.

Jim's understated observation broke seconds of stunned silence. "Well, I'm sure as hell glad we didn't follow orders and hold position."

"You got that right." Paul holstered his sidearm and shook his head. "If Hermann was in that car, where the hell is he going?"

"I don't have a clue." Jim palmed his cell phone and searched his contacts. "But I know someone who might."

Chapter 36

Escaping Chaos

Eddie searched for an opening to escape the encroaching chaos and wished for silence to help him think.

He got neither.

"Eddie!" Kelly shouted through a cell phone connection from North Side affluent safety a world away. "What's happening?"

"Where are we?" Lucas asked.

"Hey, asshole!" the driver of the taxi behind the Jeep bellowed. "Pick a fuckin' lane!"

"I would if there was one," Eddie fired back at his reflection in a window he hadn't opened. The taxi driver flipped him off. "All hell is breaking loose here, Kel."

"I can hear that," Kelly said. "Where are you?"

"That's what I want to know," Lucas repeated. "Are we near where Rayen is?"

The foul-mouthed driver blasted the taxi's horn in long bleats and staccato annoyance. A gap of daylight appeared between an idling Mini-Cooper on the left and a parked mini-van with a flat back tire. "OK, that's it." Eddie cut the wheel and floored the Jeep. The sharp right turn careening maneuver through an alley scattered skyward a piled tower of cardboard boxes.

"Watch out!" Lucas yelled. Eddie slammed on the brakes to avoid a collision with a speeding Hummer at the T-junction between buildings.

"This is nuts!" Eddie followed the wake of the retreating vehicle's exhaust and skirted the police blockade. Several minutes later, with enough city blocks in the rearview mirror between them and where they shouldn't have been, Eddie slotted the car between parking lot lines rapidly vanishing in snow. He breathed deeply to take the edge off panic. "You still there, Kel?" he asked.

"Yes, and I'm glad you are. Now can you tell me where you are and where you were?"

"I'm not exactly sure of our location at the moment." Eddie looked around for a street sign or recognizable landmark. "I think we're a couple miles east of the South Side bodega."

Lucas glared at Eddie, his eyes dark as coal. "So, we were close to Rayen."

"Yeah, we were about a block or so away. My guess is that's where the squads were headed. Possibly as backup to a raid gone wrong." Eddie raised his hands from the steering wheel in surrender and self-defense. "Before you say anything, need I remind you I was trying to turn the car around at your request?"

The hard glare retreated from his client's eyes. Lucas breathed in deeply and let it out slowly. "Victoria? Are you there?"

"Yes, Lucas," she replied. "I'm here."

"I'm sorry, but I must know what happened to Rayen."

"I know you do, love. But going back for her now is too dangerous. There has to be another way. We'll find it. Please, Lucas."

Eddie scrubbed nervous sweat from his upper lip and shoved the transmission into gear. "So, what's it gonna be? It's your call, man."

The internal struggle to act receded. His shoulders dropped as he sunk back into the seat. "Victoria is right," Lucas conceded. "We'll find another way."

"Wise choice." Eddie steered the Jeep out of the parking lot and onto the comparative quiet of a residential side street.

Chapter 37

The Favor

The cell phone rang as Cecily ripped the dealer's sold sign off the windshield of the new to her older model Chevy Blazer. She grinned at the name that flashed on caller ID. "Hey, Jim," she answered. "Are you finally gonna ask me out? By my count, you've been legally free for six years. A girl won't wait forever."

"Gee, I didn't know you cared," Ross replied. "Tempting, but that's not why I called." His quick synopsis of the failed raid concluded with a plea. "If you know where Hermann might go to hole up with a hostage, I need to hear it now."

Cecily's spine stiffened against the red leather driver's seat. "Why would I know that?"

"Don't bullshit me. I know you've been keeping track of that mutt since Kelly's brother was murdered. You thought you had him dead to rights. Then the DA's office screwed up, and he walked on a technicality." Cecily heard a woman's voice complain about time wasted. "C'mon. Help me out here."

Her cell phone chirped an incoming call alert. "Give me a few minutes to think about it. I'll call you back." Cecily ended one call and took the other. "Yeah, Kelly, what's up?"

"Eddie and Lucas got caught in the middle of a Chicago PD shit show in the neighborhood where Rayen is," Kelly told her friend.

"Yeah, I heard about that. I just talked to Jim," Cecily said. "Did Eddie know about the raid? I can't believe Jim would tell him."

"He didn't. They just happened to be near there when it went down."

"Why do I find that hard to believe?"

"Kelly?" she heard Tori say. "Why is this dot moving?"

"Hang on a second." Familiar sounds of movement sifted through the cell phone connection. "Cec!" she relayed through the phone. "Lucas's laptop has been turned on!"

"Rayen must have gotten the note," Cecily said. "Tell me where it is."

"Heading north on South Kedzie. Just turned right on West Ogden." She groaned. "Aw Cec, that's a teeny needle and a lot of haystacks to hide it in."

"Yes and no. Where are Eddie and Lucas?"

"On their way back to the penthouse."

"I've gotta call Jim back. This is important, Kelly. Don't say anything to Eddie until I call you back."

"Wait! Cec! Tell me where …"

Cecily hung up on Kelly and redialed Jim. "Talk to me," he answered.

"The laptop is on."

"Tell me something I don't know."

"You know that brewery that was shuttered a couple months back?"

"Go on."

"The DA suspected Hermann was running drugs and human trafficking sex for sale out of there but couldn't prove it. It was temporarily closed down on an old disorderly house rule left over from Prohibition. I'd stake my reputation on a hunch that's where he's taking Rayen and the laptop."

"If he finds out the laptop is on, he's got what he wants."

"And she's dead. You gotta move fast. But go in light and easy on the backup, or he'll run to another hole."

"Got it. Thanks. I owe you dinner."

***

An unlikely team of law enforcement officers with different goals tied to a similar purpose huddled on the rooftop. Braced flat-footed and shoulder-width apart against Windy City gusts and the fat splat of wet snowflakes from a rapidly approaching storm.

"My contact has a location." Jim gestured toward the wreckage below. "Obviously we need a unit to get there." His gaze met the Canadians' watery from the cold stare. "You with us?"

"How reliable is this source?" Agent Cartier asked.

"Very," Jim replied. "She knows Hermann's profile better than anyone. She says we should do this alone and go now. Too much backup would tip him off, and we'd be back at square one or worse. No laptop and a dead hostage."

"How will we leave the scene without alerting one of your commanding officers?" Inspector Freeland asked.

"Leave that to me." Jim turned and led his team down three flights of stairs. "Look for Bill Collier," he said to his partner on the way down. "He owes me a favor or three." Paul spotted the sergeant directing incoming and outgoing medic gurney traffic on the first floor.

Collier smirked at Jim's request for immediate transportation in an unmarked car. "Ross, you know it's my ass if I do an end run around another CO," the sergeant replied. "How much backup do you need?"

"None."

Collier's eyebrows lifted. "Also, not kosher."

"Bill, I wouldn't ask if I didn't think we had a chance. We've got this runner cornered. I know we can put him away for good."

Collier's gaze locked for a moment with the cop he'd known since their first day on the street. "That's good enough for me." The sergeant strode out the front door to the street, and the unmarked parked at the curb. "Detective Ross needs this vehicle," he said to the officer in the driver's seat. "Give him the keys."

Chapter 38

Follow that dot!

The redial to Cecily went straight to voicemail. Kelly swore at the phone in her hand and resisted the urge to throw something else within reach.

"What's happening?" The pool in Tori's teary green eyes reflected a twined knot of anxiety and fear that threatened to unravel.

I've got to give her something to do. "Tori, I need your help." Kelly rolled out the desk chair. "Watch the screen. Don't take your eyes off that dot."

Tori sat on the edge of the seat, her feet flat on the floor. "What are you going to do?"

"Go where the moving dot leads." Kelly tried Cecily's number again with the same voicemail result. "Use the landline phone on my desk to call me. Tell me when and where it moves, which street it turns on, and in what direction. Can you do that for me?"

"What about Eddie and Lucas?"

"I'm getting to that," Kelly called the Jeep's driver. "Where are you?"

"Not far from home," Eddie replied. Sounds of the city thrummed through the connection.

"Don't park. Pull in out front. Send Lucas up. I'm on my way down." Kelly slipped into a navy blue down parka and slid her hands into matching wool gloves. "We're counting on you. Watch that dot."

"I will, and I am."

Kelly redialed Cecily as the descending elevator ticked past numbered floors. "I can't talk now. I'll call you when I can."

"Does Hermann have the laptop and Rayen?"

"Not sure."

"What's his destination?"

"Can't tell you that, either."

"You could, but you won't. Fine by me. We'll see who gets there first."

"No! Stay out of this! I know what Hermann is capable of. What he's done, you don't! Kelly, please listen to ..."

Kelly ended the call at ground level. "Two can play this game, sista." She stepped through the open doors and out into the dark, the cold, and the savage swirl of icy snow. The Jeep lurched to a stop under the protective canopy. Kelly rounded the back bumper and opened the passenger side door. "OK, Lucas, we'll take it from here."

The seatbelt stayed buckled. Lucas didn't move. He stared straight ahead through the swipe of wipers on the defrosting windshield. "I'm going with you."

"Uh, no." Kelly stomped her feet for emphasis and warmth. "You're not."

His air of defiance abruptly ceased the visible puffs of her warm breath. "Unless you plan to somehow remove me from this car by force, I suggest you join us."

"Well, I never," Kelly sputtered.

"Forget it, Kel," Eddie said. "Lucas and I have already had this conversation. "He's made up his mind."

Kelly folded her long legs behind the seat Lucas refused to vacate and closed the car door. "Tori won't like this," she grumbled.

"Rayen is my responsibility," Lucas said. "I have to go to her. Victoria will understand."

The cell phone in Kelly's coat pocket vibrated. "We're about to find out." She answered. "Where is the dot now, Tori?"

"Turning right on Washtenaw Avenue, and where is Lucas? Is he in the elevator?"

Kelly held up her phone between the seats. "It's for you."

148

"Victoria, I ..."

"You're going to risk your life again to save her." Tori's flat tone trailed through the phone. "Can everyone hear me?"

Eddie transferred the signal to hands-free. "We can now."

"The dot isn't moving anymore," Tori said. "It went left on west seventeenth street and stopped behind a building about three or four blocks east of Washtenaw."

Eddie steered the car south. The honk of horns, skidding tires, and accelerating engines filled tense moments of strained silence until Tori spoke again. "Be careful. Don't do anything stupid. And don't hang up! I want to know what's happening."

"We'll stay with you," Kelly assured her.

"For as long as we can," Eddie added.

"I'll be with you always, mon amour," Lucas said.

"You'd better. I want to be your wife. I want that wedding, a white dress with yards of lace and real pearls, a giant bouquet of lilies, a diamond ring to die for, to be Canadian, learn French, and fall asleep in your arms every night until the day I die." Tori tried to stifle a sob with a cough. "Je t'aime, Lucas. Please come back for me."

Chapter 39

Unexpected Backup

"Thank you." Paul intercepted the keys tossed by the exiting officer and buckled in behind the steering wheel.

"Hey!" Jim protested. "Who said you could drive?"

Paul turned the key in the ignition and glanced in the rearview and side mirrors. "I know the shortest routes, I can get us there faster, and I'm a better driver, especially in these conditions."

"But I know where we're going," Jim countered.

"So do they," Paul nodded at the Canadian officers in the back seat engaged in conversation on a shared open cell phone line. "Tell me where to go."

"Love to," Jim grumbled and got in.

Paul lit up the unmarked and steered through the maze of ambulances, marked squads, and civilians in vehicles and on foot. Blown snow pelted the windshield, swept clear by wipers, then covered in seconds. Paul aimed the tires to follow tracks laid down by snowplows on primary streets and carved new paths on side roads travelers avoided.

"Detective," Inspector Freeland said, "the laptop is stationary. Location pinpointed. Twenty-six hundred block, west seventeenth street."

"That's the boarded-up brewery," Jim said, whistling through his teeth. "Damn, she's good." He turned around and stretched the seatbelt's limit. "Tell the Consulate General to shut down that computer."

"Excuse me?" Freeland's narrowed eyes stared between the lines of the grid barrier between the front and back seats.

"Agreed," Agent Cartier said. She spoke a few words in French into the cell phone. "If the suspect knows we know where he is, he'll run."

"And we'd have a dead hostage on our hands." Jim squinted into the surrounding reality of Chicago's South Side snow globe. "What the hell." Interior condensation the defroster couldn't quite clear fogged his view of the car ahead. "Who the hell." He wiped the sleeve of his coat on the windshield. "Can you make out the plate?" he asked his partner.

"Yup." Paul read it out loud. "Call it in," he said.

"Way ahead of you," Jim replied and cursed the verified registration of the owner. "Well, of course, it is."

***

Cecily eased her foot on and off the brake. The Chevy skid in rubber grinding slow spin contact with curbed concrete, then crept to a crawl around the corner. Down a snow-jammed street toward a boarded-up brewery. "Dammit." She cursed at the voicemail from Kelly's phone and killed the headlights.

Streetlight beams on a vacant property refracted the curved outline of a stationary object white as nature's winter confetti. "Dammit!" Cecily pumped the pedal and held her breath. The living portrait framed in the car door window, her front bumper nearly kissed, reacted in shadowed motions. Eyes wide. Mouth opened in a silent shout.

Fuck if you didn't get here first, Eddie. Headlights in her rearview mirror flashed, then faded to dim in approach. Cecily's cell phone chattered in the console slot between cup holders.

"So, you just had to stick your nose up our asses." Cecily couldn't tell if Jim was angry, amused, or both.

"Well, I'm not the only one. I almost hit a white Jeep."

***

"Shit," Jim groaned and hung up.

"Now what?" Paul asked while Jim's thumb flicked the screen on his phone in search of a contact.

"We've got more baggage than an unclaimed auction at O'Hare." Jim tapped the screen.

Eddie answered in mid-tone. "Jim, I know what you're gonna say."

"Then do it. Go home."

"We're here. Not happening."

"Have it your way. I'm placing you and Kelly under arrest for interfering with a police investigation."

"You can handcuff us. But you can't touch our client. Diplomatic immunity."

"Dominguez is with you?"

"He is. He insisted, and he won't leave without Rayen."

"Great," Jim grumbled. "Just great."

"I've got a plan," Eddie said.

"I'll bet you do," Jim retorted.

"Wait. Hear me out," Eddie said. "I go in with Lucas."

"I hate it." Jim scrubbed his chin with his free hand. "Hang on, and don't hang up." Jim kept the line open. "Your diplomat is in the car ahead of the one in front of us," he told the Canadian officers. "He's with the private investigators he hired to find Rayen Vasquez."

"Mr. Dominguez must be removed from the scene," Agent Cartier said. "Inspector Freeland will secure the laptop."

"Dominguez won't go without Rayen," Jim explained.

"I will convince him that he has to. Unlock my door, detective." The CSIS agent stepped out of the car and into the storm.

"Heads up, Eddie," Jim spoke into the phone.

"Yeah, we heard."

***

Eddie spotted the advancing officer, an imposing figure of dark blue determination cutting through a near blizzard. The cold blast intrusion through the open back door spit in snow and dropped the temperature several degrees.

"Agent Cartier, Canadian Security Intelligence Service."

Kelly brushed winter from her coat and the car seat. "Kelly Gillespie, and this is my partner."

"We don't have time to exchange pleasantries." Agent Cartier turned her attention to the VIP citizen she was sworn to protect. "Sir, you must leave now. A police escort of this vehicle will take you to a safe location."

"Now, hold on," Kelly protested. "This is our car, and you can't just commandeer it."

The agent's steeled precision focused briefly on Kelly. "I can, and I will."

"I thank you for your concern, and I understand your duty and obligation to me." Lucas countered her take charge tone with his calm strength. "I'm not going anywhere until I know Rayen is safe. When that happens, I will comply with your request, and Rayen and I will leave together."

"I'm sorry, sir, but that is unacceptable." Agent Cartier held up her cell phone. "I am in contact with the Consulate General, who supports my assessment and agrees with the directive."

Lucas turned squared shoulders and a firm expression of resolved resistance to confront the CSIS agent. "I am prepared to resign my position with the Consulate General and the Government of Canada if that's what I must do to save Rayen."

The static of confrontation in the confined space crackled like an electric charge before the lightning strike. Eddie let out the breath he'd been holding. "Jim," he said into his cell phone, "did you?"

"Hear that. Yeah."

***

Jim looked at Paul. "Refresh my memory. Didn't Dominguez say the guy in Buenos Aires who told him to get the next flight out warned him not to involve the police?"

Paul nodded. "He also said he knew Lucas was Canadian."

153

"Are you thinking what I'm thinking?"

"That Hermann's extending his reach, and the dirty hands on both ends are holding badges," Paul said.

"Yeah, that's what I'm thinking." Jim thumped his fist on the dashboard. "OK, Eddie," he said into the cell phone. "I'll still hate it. Now tell me your plan."

Chapter 40

The Plan

Urgent consensus reached by cell phone link between passengers in the first and last vehicles to arrive left Cecily in the middle and out of the loop.

"Hey!" The swipe and hollow thump of her gloved hand and knuckles on the car window got Jim's attention. "I'm freezing out here! Unlock the damn door."

"It's open," he shouted from behind the glass.

She jerked the door open, plopped, and slammed herself in beside a man in a uniform she didn't recognize. "Who the hell are you?"

"I ask you the same question." Inspector Freeland brushed windblown snow off the arms and crested crown shoulder patch on his coat.

"Well, a real live Mountie. Cecily Vosh," she answered and gestured to Jim, "formerly his partner, now a trial science lawyer, always a pain in the ass and the best shot you all have at taking Hermann down without a body count." She peered around the grid and exchanged glances with Jim and Paul. "Since every call I made went to voicemail, I assume there is a plan. So, what have we got?"

"Everything but a way in without being seen or heard," Jim answered.

"The snow and wind will cancel out the sound, and any main floor windows are likely boarded up," Paul observed. "If a couple of us split up, we could circle the building to spot the most vulnerable entry point."

"But we have no idea where Hermann could be in that building," Inspector Freeland noted. "That's a tough call without knowing the layout."

"I think I can help with that." Cecily scrolled images on her cell phone. "I took a photo of the blueprints when the assistant DA prosecuting the case against the brewery owner conveniently stepped out of his office."

"How did you manage to muscle your way into that opportunity?" Jim asked.

She turned the phone around for group viewing. "With a bag of donuts and a large caramel latte."

Jim snorted through a half-grin. "Sweet."

"The loading bay doors open on an area that is very exposed," Cecily explained. "There are two points of entry around back, off the main parking lot. One is for Brew Room customers, the other for employees. Both doors open to hallways. The employee door hallway leads to the brewery. The Brew Room is in the middle of the building, but the brewery can be accessed from the bar."

Jim studied the cell phone image and looked back at Cecily. "Where would Hermann be holding Rayen?" he asked her.

"Possibly in the Brew Room. Maybe the brewery."

"He'd want a place away from marked exits," Paul said. "If Rayen were in the Brew Room and got away, she could make a break for one of the exits in the back," Paul said. "I'd say those doors are our best way in. If he's got her in the brewery, we can use the vats as cover."

"OK, so how do we get in?" Inspector Freeland asked.

"The first trick just about every PI shoves up their sleeve is how to pick a lock," Jim replied. "I'm sure Eddie is no exception."

"But he'll come in with Dominguez after us," Paul reminded his partner.

"What about his partner?" Freeland asked.

Jim rubbed his chin. "I'm not sure if that's in Kelly's skill set."

Cecily huffed out a snort. "Are you kidding me? Every time I locked myself out of the Camaro or my apartment, I called Kelly," Cecily remarked. "I never had to call a locksmith. She probably showed Eddie how it's done."

"I was hoping to keep Kelly out of this," Jim said. "Too many moving parts and unarmed targets."

"That's bullshit, Jim!" Cecily protested. "Kelly swung a baseball bat and dropped an assassin who would have killed you."

"I know. I wouldn't have believed it if I wasn't there," Jim replied. "But to be honest, neither you nor Kelly were part of the plan."

Cecily's eyes narrowed. Her cheeks flushed. "There is no way you're gonna kick me to the curb on this one. I've been doggin' this low life since you had a full head of hair. Hermann is my collar!"

"He was once," Jim said. "Not now."

"Excuse me," the RCMP officer interrupted. "This is your investigation and your call. But," he turned to Cecily beside him, "you were a detective. Are you still licensed to carry?"

"You bet your ass I am," she replied, "and I never leave home unarmed."

Freeland looked from Paul to Jim on the other side of the grid barrier. "Then I say we need all the hands and help we can get."

Jim frowned and shook his head. "I hope I don't live to regret this." He pressed the cell phone to his ear. "Did you get all of that?" he asked Eddie.

"Loud and clear," Eddie answered.

"Ready?"

***

"As we'll ever be." Eddie nodded to Lucas. Agent Cartier took the cue to join her fellow officer in flank position ahead of Lucas.

"I hate this." Kelly reached between the Jeep's front seats and caught Eddie's coat sleeve. "I love you. Please, please be careful."

Eddie leaned over the leather and kissed her. "I will, and I love you, too." The car's back door opened within seconds of his side-by-side stride with Lucas toward the semi-dark and shuttered warehouse.

Cecily slid in and settled where Cartier had been. "OK, girlfriend," she said to Kelly. "Here's what we're gonna do."

***

Dragon prowled the catwalk above the covered vats and chimney stacks that connected a row of upside-down stainless-steel cones to the concave arch-beamed ceiling. Light from bulbs in the few working overhead fixtures struggled to chase away the dim. Tall thin slivers of sealed windows on the far end of the building above the Brew Room broke walled monotony on the front and back sides of the stilled brewery. The pungent stench of soured hops, barley and aged burger grease permeated stagnant, barely breathable air warmed just enough to keep pipes from freezing.

"Bring your ass down here and pull up a piece of floor." Hermann's raspy voice echoed from the lowest level in the concrete chamber. "You're making me nervous."

"I can't see out from down there."

"There's nothing to see. Nobody knows we're here."

Dragon walked past and glanced out the glass between the boards. He saw figures and shadows advancing through the storm. And froze. "Oh, yeah? They do."

"What! Who?"

"Can't tell." Dragon squinted his eyes and stared into a sideways blown curtain of white. "Is that computer on?"

Hermann scooped up the laptop from the concrete floor next to his backside and opened the lid to a dark screen. "No."

"Then how the fuck?" Dragon trotted down the stairs. He looked around and saw only Hermann squatted in a crumpled heap. "Where is she?"

Hermann lurched to his feet. "Tied up in the Brew Room."

"Fucking idiot," Dragon hissed under his breath. "Are you sure?" Wide strides on long legs spanned the space between where beer had been made for customers no longer seated on bar stools and around tables. Dragon kicked open the divided swinging doors that sectioned off the warehouse from food and drink prep and service. A bottle thrown from behind the bar missed his head and exploded on impact with the brick exterior wall. He pivoted toward the rapid foot slap of a run to escape. His legs tangled with an overturned bar stool. He fell hard into broken glass. Blood oozed from a sharp shard embedded in his palm.

"You bitch!" Dragon yanked the glass from his hand, scrambled to his feet, kicked a chair prone in his path, and heaved the stool over the bar. Every long and round table obstacle she tried to put between them failed to slow his advance. Rayen broke away and ran for her life down the dark corridor of dead neon ribbons.

Dragon captured her under the glowing red and white exit sign. The muscles in his forearm tightened around her neck and silenced the terrified scream. Rayen clawed at the tatoo's talons and wheezed in strangled breaths.

"I'd kill you now, chica," he threatened, "but we have unfinished business. You are the bait that will reel in the big fish." He tightened his grip and dragged her back through the Brew Room doors into the bowels of the brewery.

"Do you think you can manage to control her with this?" Dragon let go of his prisoner. Rayen dropped in a heap at Hermann's feet. Dragon drew the blade that had bested Perez.

Rage replaced Hermann's surprise at the blue-lipped loose, barely conscious hostage. He wrapped his right hand around the hilt and turned the weapon over in his left. "I'll handle her. What are you gonna do?"

Dragon caressed the pearl-handled Smith and Wesson he'd lifted from the belted holster secured at the small of his back. "Target practice."

Chapter 41

Gaining Entry

The conquered padlock separated in the protected palm of Kelly's fingerless gloves. Drifted snow swallowed the discarded, useless chain. Kelly coaxed a razor-thin pointed tool into the round lock and pressed her ear against frigid metal. "Personal best," she proclaimed seconds later and stepped away behind Cecily's armed protection.

Jim and Paul bracketed the liberated door. Backs against the wall. Eyes on each other. The employee entry door eased open with Paul's pull. A scream from the other side collided with the wind's taunting whistle.

"Rayen!" Lucas pivoted from the planned separate point of entry. He broke away from his protectors and headed toward the scream.

"Shit!" Eddie's short sprint on the thick tread grip of his boots provided the traction he needed to intercept his client on shifting terrain. He blocked Lucas with his body. Fingers in gloved hands dug into the larger man's shoulders.

"We go in last." Eddie's in-his-face reminder quelled resistance. "You've got to let them do their job first."

Lucas looked away from the distant door over Eddie's stiff shoulder. Their gaze met and held. *He knows in his head, but his heart doesn't think.* Eddie flinched at the intensely desperate pain in the exchange.

Lucas raised his gloved hand to Eddie's shoulder and nodded. Cartier and Freeland closed the gap and moved in close to guard their country's diplomat against any threat of imminent danger.

Jim stepped over the framed threshold; his weight balanced equally on the rubber tread soles of his boots. He pointed the barrel of his sidearm ahead into the dim unknown and motioned for Paul to follow.

***

Anticipation fired Dragon's adrenal cylinders. The catwalk lured him like a web littered with twitching live food for a ravenous spider. He took the steps two-at-a-time. Quiet. The balls of his feet were like the pads on a cat's paw. A sudden shot of cold air rippled the hairs on his wrists and forearms. He crouched. Saw the door open. Waited.

A bare balding head appeared under a single bulb screwed into a canister imbedded in the warehouse ceiling. Flak jacket worn under the open zipper of a Chicago PD parka. Arms extended. Standard issue Glock ready to protect or defend.

Another cop. Skull cap snug from forehead to neckline. Younger. Less bulk. More agile. Same alert stance.

Chapped lips stretched over crooked front teeth. Dragon's tongue licked the dry grin. *Come to papa.*

He rested his wrist on the catwalk's metal bar. The pearl handle silky smooth and steady in his hand. The barrel of the gun aimed on targets below.

***

Cecily kept the door from closing. Her booted foot jammed, caught, and held the weight of the metal. She ignored the pinch of pain. Cinched the narrow B-width opening wider with her thigh. Shoved her shoulder inside. Senses on full alert searched for movement. A pot light beam illuminated facial features Cecily instantly recognized.

Fucking hell! She held her weapon at arm's length in both hands and prepared for battle.

Kelly tugged at her friend's coat sleeve. "Other lock," she mouthed in silence.

Cecily shook her off. Her lips formed the word. "Go." She bent her knees level to the fallen snow and crept in from the cold. The closing door tapped the heel of her boot.

***

Kelly fingered the torsion wrench and lock pick in her palm. Her fist and teeth clenched in frustration over a plan with a gaping hole.

Damn you, Cec!

The advancing Canadian officers took point with weapons drawn. Ready for Cecily to lead the way and back them up.

What am I gonna tell them?

Eddie and Lucas followed in side-by-side formation, confident that Kelly would coax another lock open without a key.

Shit!

Kelly slipped on black ice invisible under six inches of white. The parka padded her fall. Recesses and protrusions in the building's façade served as finger and handholds to steady her on the way up and forward. Onward around the sharply right-angled corner to a wall without windows and the padlock on a double-hung metal door.

Snow sifted through gaps in the metal pergola canopy where they converged around Kelly, each with the same unspoken question.

Where is Cecily?

Kelly pointed toward the door. *Inside.*

The shackle loop slid, and the freed chain fell. Kelly's wrench and pick manipulated the lock's pins.

Eddie signaled his plan B. Held up his left hand, palm forward. Pointed as Kelly had with the trigger finger on his right. *I say. Go in.*

Agent Cartier's eyes narrowed and shifted in confirmation to her RCMP counterpart. Inspector Freeland's chin dipped an affirming nod. The officers raised their weapons.

Kelly gripped the handle and pulled. The door eased open.

***

Every other odd, shaded bulb dangling on a wire strung from the high ceiling was as dark as the tubes of neon mounted on the long hallway walls. Straight yellow arrows and flowing blue waves beckoned no one to down a beer at the bar or order a round at a table in the Brew Room ahead, marked in red.

Jim hunched in deep shadowy pockets between weak pools of overhead light. Knees bent. Left hand under the right, held the weapon steady. He blinked to help his eyes adjust and search for movement. The ever-present and always annoying tinnitus buzz in his head was the only sound Jim heard in the otherwise deafening silence.

The detectives breached the Brew Room threshold together. Their back-to-back opposing shoulders touched in defensive V-stance.

"Only saw the Humvee." Jim strained to hear Paul's observation spoken barely above a whisper. "You?"

"Could be more in the bays inside up front." Jim glanced around the dining room. Chairs seat down and flat on tables. Wooden legs raised high and straight in empty surrender.

"I doubt Hermann drove off without backup."

"He couldn't."

"Why not?"

"Doesn't drive."

"That's weird."

"Is it? Think. He keeps his gun in a drawer. Never carries."

"Huh."

Jim couldn't tell if Paul had rubbed his chin. But he half-grinned at his partner's borrow of the senior detective's go-to, think-it-through habit.

"Makes it tougher to get convictions. Can't drive. Not armed. No trail. Less evidence." Paul's peripheral vision caught the light that spilled across the floor in a triangle pattern through a partially open door marked for employees only. He tapped Jim on the shoulder. Pointed at and stepped toward a broken chair. Looked down at the glass that crunched under his boots. Heard the hammer pull on a single-action revolver. Looked up. Saw the catwalk. The coiled menace in black. The silver gun barrel gleamed between the metal rails.

Paul spun and shoved his partner.

Jim scrambled for cover under the nearest table and cursed his aching knees.

***

Eddie watched the Canadians duck and dodge stealth maneuver through a maze of vats that looked like upside-down steel popsicles on sticks that stretched to the ceiling. The round glass in the swinging door between the narrow, dingy, gray hallway and the expansive brewery framed his face like a collar-to-crown portrait for a locket. Eddie backed away from the door Agent Cartier and Inspector Freeland pushed quietly through.

"There's a line of tall wooden barrels in front of the steel vats," Freeland said.

"Rayen's sitting on the floor with her back against a barrel about ten meters from the closed bay doors. Her hands are tied behind her. She's gagged by a man's tie. The laptop is under his arm. He's pacing the floor in front of her."

"Is he armed?" Eddie asked.

"Not that we could see," Cartier replied.

Lucas unfurled fists that had tightened during Freeland's description of Rayen's plight. He breathed in deep. His shoulders visibly relaxed with the breath he expelled. The pool of calm in his eyes reflected confidence. "Let's go," he said to Eddie.

Agent Cartier stopped his reach for the door. "Sir, I don't support this course of action."

Lucas turned to the CSIS officer. The control required of a career diplomat tempered the intensity of his determination. "Agent Cartier, your duty is to me. Mine is to Rayen."

Freeland flattened his hand on the door. He pushed it open. Lucas nodded his thanks, crossed over, and onward in a straight line alongside Eddie.

Cartier and Freeland raised their weapons and retraced their steps around the vats to protect Lucas and retrieve the stolen portal to Canadian national security.

Chapter 42

A Verbal Showdown

Eddie ran through the lines and scene agreed upon to confront Hermann and decided to chuck it all. Improvise. He peeled off and stuffed damp gloves in his coat pockets. He wiped palm sweat on his pant legs. *Breathe. You can do this.* Eddie circled the last vat bastion of cover and stepped in front of Lucas. Hermann reversed his pace away from them.

"Hey." *Hey?! That's all you got?* "Hello." *What an idiot!*

The career criminal whirled. Glared at Eddie. A soul-chilling depth of ice-blue cold that rivaled Chicago winter. The scars on his face stretched with the lip-lift sneer.

Eddie felt the hair rise on the back of his neck. He swallowed. Hard.

"Who the fuck are you?" Hermann advanced. "How did you get in here?"

Make it good. Eddie forced a smile. "I'm a private investigator. I pick locks." He lifted his arms in surrender. *And then what?* "My client and I were on our way to see you." Eddie forced a few seconds delay laugh.

Hermann grunted in disgust or disbelief. Eddie couldn't tell which. "How did you find me?"

Truth? "Your Humvee almost hit my car in the alley. I took a chance you were in it and followed you here." *But not the whole truth.*

Hermann's narrowed eyes shifted from Eddie to Lucas. "This your client?"

"It is."

"Bullshit!" Hermann vice-grip hugged the laptop to his chest. "You look and smell like cops."

"We're not cops." Eddie opened his coat wide. "No guns. No badges. My private investigator license is in my jacket pocket. I'll get it out and show you."

"Fuck that." Hermann stepped toward Lucas. "What do you want?"

"An exchange." Lucas stared at Hermann. His voice held steady. "You have my laptop. I alone know the passcode. I give that to you. You release Rayen to me."

Rayen reacted to the sound of him. The words pronounced in English with a hint of homeland. She lifted her chin from her chest and bit the fabric in her mouth. She struggled to free her hands from the tangled knots. Her eyes dark as his, red-rimmed from exhaustion and tears, flickered in fright. Shone with hope.

Eddie noticed Lucas' hand twitch. *My God, this must be killing him.*

Hermann spit out a joyless laugh. "So, you're the big shot diplomat from Canada. Poking your nose where it doesn't belong." He snorted and spit for real. "Boludo."

"I'm curious. Why do you use that word? You are not Argentine."

"You know nothing about me!"

"I make it a point to know my adversary, Octavio Hernandez."

"That is not my name!"

"It was."

"No! He's dead. I killed him." Hermann's cheeks flushed. The scar did not. "You give me the passcode. I give you Vasquez's whore daughter?" His crooked finger pointed at Rayen. The gag smothered her whimper and sob. "Why, boludo. Why do you want her? Why did you go all the way to Buenos Aires to ask questions about her and her mother?"

"Adriana Ruiz de Vasquez is a Canadian citizen. Rayen's grandmother had applied for visas …"

"More bullshit!" Hermann's face blazed red hot. "Her grandmother is dead!" He tucked the laptop under his arm and resumed pacing. "You know what I think? I think you went back to your home country as a spy. You weren't looking for his whore wife and daughter. You wanted to find Vasquez." Hermann prowled in a tight circle as if he were following a yellow brick road only he could see. The tighter the circle, the louder his rant became. "Drugs. Guns. Women. I'm losing money because of you." His road abruptly ended with Rayen. He squatted in front of his prisoner and squeezed her jaw. "She knows how much I hate losing money and what I'll do to get it back."

The crack of a single shot fired decreased the already slim chance of a peaceful outcome.

***

The bullet ricocheted off the hard surface at the spot where Jim had just left boot prints in the dust.

"Enzo De Leon."

The name spoken by a woman echoed in the vast high-ceilinged chamber of mostly cement, metal, and stainless steel.

Who the hell is that? Paul cautiously crawled between tables on his belly and elbows to discover the source Jim had instantly identified. *Cecily! What the hell are you doing?*

"Go ahead. Give me another reason to blow your sorry ass to bits." Hard surfaces created the illusion of a voice amplified in surround sound.

Jim made eye contact with his partner. "Is she up there?" he asked in a voice just above a whisper.

Paul's nod and upward air jab of his gun's barrel confirmed the location of the drama and danger.

"I know who you are. The slimiest scum on the street. A traitor with a badge." Cecily's disembodied voice seemed to move closer to the shooter's location.

"Did I hear her right?" Jim asked Paul. "De Leon works undercover narcotics in Collier's house. What the fuck is he doing hanging with Hermann?"

"Crossing more than one line apparently," Paul replied.

Cecily continued to taunt Dragon, his true identity revealed. ""Who else is on to you? Your CO? Your boss man Hermann? You can play those fools, Detective De Leon. But not me. Uh-uh. No way."

Jim shifted position and glanced up at the catwalk. "Is it the echo? Or did she turn up the volume?"

Paul looked up at the wide-open space to the metal roof. "Everyone in this building can hear what she's saying."

"Including Hermann."

"Especially Hermann."

Jim winced at the pain in his hips from lying on the cold, unyielding concrete floor and envisioned brilliant sunshine on lush green links. *I'm way too old for this crap.* "Stands to reason there's got to be a way up there."

"How about we split up," Paul suggested. "First one to find the stairs has Cecily's back. The other backs up Cartier and Freeland."

"Copy that." Jim watched as his partner cut across the hallway and slipped through the crease of a door left ajar.

Backup. Jim called Kelly on his cell phone. "You OK?" she asked.

"All good except for my cold ass," Jim complained. "You in the Jeep?"

"Yes. Should I call this in?"

"Now's the time."

"Done. I put a bug in Eddie's coat pocket. They're up front with Hermann and Rayen by the bay doors."

Jim ended the call and crawled under a row of long tables to a galley kitchen behind the bar. "Bingo," he muttered when he spotted a dimly lit narrow staircase.

Cecily's voice pierced the silence. "A dirty cop screwing over his boss man. Won't go well for you in prison."

"Shut up, bitch!" De Leon's verbal distress boomed down the tunnel that led Jim up.

"What's in it for you, De Leon? Contraband? Cash? Start a turf war? Take over when Hermann goes down? All of the above?"

"That's my girl. Keep talking." Jim cheered her on under his breath and began the climb.

Chapter 43

War of Words

Reactions down below reverberated with the shock of gunfire. Rayen folded herself into a knot as tight as the bindings behind her back.

Hermann crouched on his heels next to her, his arms wrapped around the laptop he also held hostage. The foreign name spoken by a voice he didn't know confused him. "Who is that?"

Eddie fought to control the lightning bolt of fear that rocked him. He couldn't think of a good lie. *Here goes another half-truth.* "An associate from my agency." His raised hands signaled stop! wait! to the Canadian officers in his line of sight tucked behind steel vats. "She's with us." *He better buy it. I've got nothing else to sell.*

Lucas hadn't moved. "Octavio." His voice was steady, confident, and calm. "We both know what it's like to be forced from our home country. Taken away from everything familiar to us. Lost. Confused. Tormented by a past that abandoned us. But it has not. The past is still with us, Octavio."

Herman's confusion contorted to rage. "That's not my name!"

"It will always be. No matter how far removed we are from our past, it's always there, Octavio. It cannot be changed. It is who we are."

Hermann spit at Lucas and the mention of a name he despised. "No. He was weak. He trusted. He was stolen and sold!" Random words spoken in a woman's voice filtered down from the catwalk and snared Hermann's attention. *Traitor. Dirty Cop. Fools.*

The growl from his soul, spawned by the long-buried pain of deception, projected to a roar. "No one betrays Otto Hermann! No one!" Dragon's knife, concealed in the fabric of Hermann's coat sleeve, appeared in his hand. With a twisted flick of his wrist, Rayen's wrists were freed. Hermann flattened the laptop against her chest, forced her to hold on to what she'd once hoped to deliver, and roughly wrenched her upright. Rayen wobbled on her feet, unsteady and unable to escape or defend herself from the blade Hermann held at her throat.

"You want her, diplomat?" Hermann bellowed. "Tell me that passcode. Now!"

"No." Lucas lifted his arms, palms forward, elbows bent. "I will not. But I will offer myself in exchange for Rayen."

Hermann stared at Lucas. Disbelief and doubt dissolved into bewilderment. "What good is that to me?"

"The data on the laptop is encrypted. It cannot be accessed by passcode alone. Let Rayen leave with Eddie and his associate. I will stay here with you."

Lucas took two measured cautionary steps forward. "We can end this, Octavio." His gaze locked with Rayen's captor. The steady hand that reached outward motioned for Eddie to join him.

Move! Eddie forced his shaking knees to bend and his hips to respond. He clenched his teeth to ward off all possibility of chatter.

Hermann's rapid eye movements shifted from one man to the other. Sizing up the approaching enemy. Weighing the risk to survive and win another high-stakes hustle. Hermann snarled. Ripped the laptop from Rayen's hands. Tilted the sharp point of the knife at Lucas. "Fuck with me, boludo, and you're dead. Comprende?"

"Esto es entre tu y yo. This is between you and me." Lucas moved closer to the blade. "Dejala ir. Let her go."

"C'mon, Rayen." Eddie stretched his arms to her, ready to catch her if he had to.

Rayen whimpered. Threw down the tie that had gagged her. Wiped her mouth with the back of her hand. "He will kill you" were the first words she spoke to her father.

Lucas smiled at her. Tried to reassure her of what he knew to be true, but she did not. "I will be fine. Go with Eddie now."

A second shot fired on the catwalk upset the delicate balance of tension on a dangerous tightrope.

***

Cecily sensed Jim's presence on the stairs before she saw him. She knew how he'd move to back her up. Exactly as he'd taught her and she'd done to cover him. *OK. Let's take this traitor down.* She stared into the eyes of Hermann's Dragon and him into hers.

"So, tell me. When did you turn?"

"When did you? You're not a cop."

"How do I know you are if I wasn't? Riddle me that, joker."

"Joke's on you. I'm undercover."

"Yeah? Who's in bed with you? You're south of your house. Just how deep is the dirt?"

"I go where I need to."

"And do what? You knew who Perez was. You knew he was sent in to draw Hermann out. PD had him. He couldn't get away on his own. You warned him. Helped him escape. Ran with him and got behind the wheel. I seriously doubt that was your undercover assignment."

A snorted laugh huffed out between De Leon's parted lips. He spread his arms wide. "Busted." His hands came together with the gun between them. His knees bent. His heels lifted from the concrete catwalk. He spun on the soles of his shoes and aimed the barrel of the pearl-handled pistol at Jim.

Oh no, you don't! Cecily fired. De Leon clutched his left thigh. Staggered but didn't fall. Blood oozed through his fingers from the hole in his jeans.

Recognition confused and angered Jim. A detective in narcotics under Bill Collier's command? *Can't be. Collier's clean.* "Best call you can make right now is to keep your hands where we can see them and lay down your weapon."

De Leon's injured leg buckled. His bloodied hand reached out and grabbed the catwalk railing. "OK," he panted. His face contorted in a show of obvious pain. "Alright. You got me." The gun in his right hand hung barrel down in deadly suspension.

"Put it down, De Leon." Cecily circled the armed man she'd wounded, weapon ready to shoot again.

"Cecily Vosh. You are relentless." His lip curled in a humorless grimace. "We're on the same team, you know. I hate Otto Hermann as much as you do." His slow move to comply abruptly changed intent and direction. His stance squared. Wrists on the railing, he aimed his weapon at a target below.

Cecily pulled her trigger first. De Leon crumpled.

"Same team, my ass." The pearl-handled pistol Cecily kicked away skittered across the cement.

Jim flopped De Leon to his stomach and cuffed his hands. "He's not going anywhere. Go get Hermann."

"Hell yes, and hallelujah." Cecily ran for the stairs.

Chapter 44

Unscripted Drama

Paul maneuvered the maze of stainless sentries from the Brew Room doorway to a concealed advantage along the brewery wall. He watched, listened, and waited. Raised his weapon at the second gunshot. Whispered a curse and a quick prayer. *OK, people. I've had it with this. Let's finish it!*

The semi-frozen tableau of players reacted and acted on the threat of very real danger in a high-stakes, unscripted drama.

Otto Hermann looked up and away from his hostage and prey. Eddie lunged for and wrapped his arms around Rayen, spun, and toppled with her to the floor. His body shielded her from harm.

Cartier and Freeland rounded the vat they'd hidden behind and surrounded Lucas. Freeland wedged himself and the weapon he carried between their country's diplomat and the blade. Cartier demanded the laptop's return at gunpoint.

That's my cue. Paul got as close as he dared without detection.

Hermann's wild-eyed glare shifted from the cops of another country to Lucas. "You lying bastardo!" he screamed. The savage swipe of the knife sliced through the arm of Freeland's parka. Feathers spewed out and fluttered down.

Cartier's defensive kick to the groin and elbow jab broke Hermann and his nose. The knife clattered to the concrete floor.

Well, alright. Paul low whistled and holstered his gun. He pulled the metal chain and bracelets from his pocket.

Cecily grinned and winked at him. "I've waited a long time for this collar." She relieved Paul of the handcuffs. Her straight back and head held high added inches to her confident stride in boot heels. She crossed the floor and snapped the handcuffs on the semi-prone defenseless Hermann, still writhing from the sudden attack on sensitive body parts. "Read him his rights," she said to Paul.

The rise and fall howl of converging sirens confirmed Chicago's finest had arrived in force to clear the scene.

Chapter 45

Papa

"It's over, my friend."
Eddie rolled to his back and clasped the hand extended to help him
up.
"That was very brave. Thank you."
Eddie brushed the dust off his pants and jacket. "That was nothing. What
you did, changed the ending of what could have been a real shit show." Rayen
lay curled and shivering in a tightly wound self-hug cocoon. "She OK?"
"She will be." Lucas knelt beside her. Gently smoothed tangled strands that
covered abrasions and bruises of abuse and attack. "Rayen. You are safe now,"
he said. "He will never harm you again."
Rayen unfurled. Balanced her weight on trembling arms and sat up. Blinked
and stared into eyes as dark as her own. Kind eyes above a reassuring smile.
Older than the man in the photos her mother had kept hidden and shown her
the day she was sent away with the money that would get her to him. Yet
undeniably him.
"Papa!" She fell into him. Clung to him. Melted into him. Shed streams of
tears into the wool of his coat. Dug her fingers into his coat sleeves. "Papa,"
she murmured repeatedly as if to convince herself that he and this moment
were real.

Chapter 46

Sanctuary

Comforting silence settled on and within the penthouse sanctuary. Sounds of the city below couldn't rise or penetrate the luxury of insulated privacy this far above.

"Well, that was a bit of a shocker." Eddie tucked the duvet around him and Kelly.

"Not really." Kelly snuggled up, adding her warmth to his.

"Oh? How could you know something that Lucas didn't?"

"I suspected as much the first time we saw her in the Jeep's windshield."

"I don't follow," he said. "I mean, Lucas noticed the resemblance between Rayen and her mother. That's how he identified her from the photo you took."

"Maybe that's what he wanted to see. I haven't seen a photo of Adriana. Have you?"

"No. But I still don't ..."

"Look at her eyes." Kelly settled her head on Eddie's shoulder. "They are exactly like Lucas's. Same shape. Same dark as night color. But warm. Glowing. Like there's a fire burning behind them."

"Well, that's a profound and astute observation. But accurate, now that you mention it, Watson." He kissed her forehead and closed his eyes to shut out any stray sliver of impending daylight. "Let's try and get some sleep before Jim calls and wakes us all up."

***

Images in the dreamy twilight of sleep surfaced and spun out like a true crime novel Eddie had lived, not written. Lucas' questions to a stranger who claims to be his daughter. "What did you say? How can that be?" Rayen's startled stuttered cries of surprise that he didn't know. The battering and break-in of doors by a battalion of uniformed officers employing force not needed for the immobile apprehended.

The frown and deep creases in Jim's forehead when Eddie begged off trips to any station house by the PIs and their clients until morning. "C'mon, Jim, have a heart," Eddie said. "Rayen's been through hell. Lucas is in shock. Tori is back at our place waiting for news, and I'm pretty sure what she's gonna hear is not what she expects."

Jim shook his finger in Eddie's face. "I'll look the other way on one condition. Herd those cats, Eddie. Keep them under your roof. I don't want to argue with the Canadian government over diplomatic immunity. Extradition across borders is a pain in the ass, and it will be my ass if your clients leave the country."

Lucas accepted Eddie's offer of overnight accommodation and the explanation for it. Eddie slumped in the welcome warmth of the heated passenger side seat. His knowledge of Spanish limited to buying a meal and finding a place to pee, prevented him from eavesdropping on the low-volume exchange between father and daughter.

Kelly swung the Jeep under the canopy at half past three. She handed the keys over to the night staff. "I'm too tired to park it," she said, leaning on Eddie.

"That's what perks are for," he said, opening the car's back door.

Rayen's half-closed eyes opened wide. "Where are we, Papa?"

"It's alright, Rayen," Lucas reassured her. "This is where Eddie and Kelly live. We'll be staying here with them tonight."

Rayen glanced from the bright lobby to the lights of Lake Shore Drive and Lake Michigan's dark water. Her gaze followed the vertical line of the building and scattered dots of light in the windows to the top floor. "Is Victoria here?"

"Yes." Lucas looped his arm around her waist and led her through glass doors opened by doormen.

"Home at last." Eddie held the elevator door open. A small ball of furry energy bounded toward Lucas and dropped a red rubber ball at his feet.

"Hola, Cassie." Tori's arms surrounded him before he could toss the ball to her dog.

"Lucas! Mon amour! I was mad with worry! I couldn't hear what was happening. I tried calling Kelly, but I couldn't get through. All I got was her voicemail!" Her lips pressed his in a passionate kiss equally shared. Tori lay her head on his chest and opened her eyes. "Oh my!"

Rayen stared at the petite ginger-haired woman in her father's arms. "Lo siento," she said, backed away, and fixed her gaze on the plush carpet.

Eddie stepped in and tried to lighten up an awkward moment. "Mi casa es su casa. I said that right, didn't I?" The joke he tried fell flat.

Lucas's attempt to smile betrayed his exhaustion. "You did, my friend. Thank you."

"Help yourselves to anything," Eddie spoke nearly as fast as he retreated. "Food and drink in the fridge. Kel and I are just down the hall. The bedrooms up front are all yours. There are towels and robes in the bathrooms and more blankets and pillows in the closets. Should be clean clothes in the closets. Not sure of what's there exactly or the sizes. I can order up whatever you need."

Lucas held on to Tori and observed Rayen's reaction to opulence she'd likely never known. Her fingers brushed and caressed the smooth, soft leather furnishings. She eyed the front-to-back fireplaces and froze in front of the floor-to-ceiling window view of a city she'd likely never seen. "We'll be fine," Lucas said. "Goodnight, Eddie."

"And goodnight," Eddie mumbled in his sleep.

Chapter 47

The Fallout

The usual groan and buzz of the station house ebbed and crashed in unusually shrill decibel waves. The motion of sound aggravated Jim's headache. Cecily's angry retorts aimed at his commanding officer further roiled the verbal ocean.

"I'm a private citizen with a license to carry, and I didn't interfere with your operation! I finished it!" Cecily refused to sit.

Sergeant Brenda Talbot would not stand down. "Your continued unauthorized investigation of a known criminal resulted in a mistrial and put him back on the street. Your presence tonight could jeopardize this case."

"My presence tonight saved his ass," Cecily pointed at Jim, "and uncovered a dirty cop." Raw energy crackled in the tense exchange. Accusations hung in the heated air. "I'm damn sure he's not the only one."

Paul leaned over his partner's slumped shoulder. "I think you better get her out of here."

"I think you're right." Jim rolled away from his desk and stood up from the chair. "Sarge. A word, please." He motioned toward his CO's office. The glass in the door rattled at the rough close and click.

Sergeant Talbot sidestepped piles of paper in and out of folders and stood behind her desk. "I'm all out of favors, detective."

Jim raised his hands in surrender. "I know, I know. And I appreciate that. I will get statements from the PIs and their clients in the morning as promised."

"Damn straight you will." Sergeant Talbot sat but didn't slump or show any outward sign of fatigue. "I read Cecily Vosh's personnel file. She was on the verge of dismissal when she resigned."

Jim nodded. "I knew that."

"She's a loose cannon, detective."

"I know that, too. But she's right about one thing. She did save my ass tonight, and not for the first time."

"So, what is your request?"

"Let me take her home. Calm her down. We'll sort it out tomorrow."

"Sorting this out will take much longer than a day." Sergeant Talbot breathed in. Her long breath out reminded Jim of a deflating balloon. "Agreed. Go before I change my mind."

***

Jim hustled Cecily out of the station house and to his car.

"What about my car?" she demanded to know.

"Nothing will happen to it. It's parked in lockup. I'll bring you back tomorrow to get it. Now get in. I'm taking you home." Jim ignored her rant hurled at Chicago PD in general and his CO in particular from the thump of Loop traffic to the quiet of her working-class neighborhood.

Cecily unbuckled her seat belt and clutched the purse she'd wrestled from under the front seat of her car prior to departure. "Have you heard a word I've said?"

"I made a conscious effort not to." Jim turned the car off and reached for the belt he hadn't buckled. "If I ask you a question, will you give me an honest answer?"

"I've never lied to you."

"Then tell me. Why are you trying so hard to self-destruct?"

Cecily stiffened and bristled. She shot him a look to kill. "What the hell do you mean self-destruct?" She opened the car door and sank into ankle-deep snow in three-inch heels. "Fuck you!" she screamed. Metal slammed to metal. Her stomp to the front door left a trail of boot prints.

Jim's pursuit tracked larger prints in a wider stride. "I knew you had a problem from day one. Sniffing all the hydrants and lampposts. Checking for messages. You're a mixed breed cross between a bulldog and a bloodhound. Stupid, arrogant me. I thought I could train you to use that obsession to your advantage. But no! Can't tame Cecily Vosh! No way. Not a chance. She'll never learn, never listen, and God forbid ever change."

Cecily drilled the key into the lock and shoved it. The door creaked open in stiff protest. She spun on her heels. Faced the street and Jim. "I don't have a problem. I look until I find the truth, and that pisses people off. I have twenty-twenty vision. Can I help it if the rest of the world needs a white cane and a seeing-eye dog?"

"Oh, and I suppose I'm blind."

"You don't see me." Her fists curled in the fabric of his department-issue jacket. Her arms pulled him over her doorstep. "But I see you. And you're so damn sexy when you're angry."

The force of her kiss shocked his world.

Chapter 48

Processing Emotions

Memories, both distant and fresh in his mind, wouldn't let Lucas sleep. Dusty streets, suffocating heat, and his mother's screams gave way to the glare of black ice on concrete and the mournful moan of a city in pain. Red and gold ribbons shimmered in a cascade of braids and waves he remembered well. The child beside her reached for him, looked up at him with eyes like his own, and called him Papa.

"Can't sleep?"

Green eyes, bright as dew-covered grass on a spring morning, gazed into his. His fingers brushed hair the color of burning embers from skin smooth as ivory silk. *My beautiful one. My Victoria.*

"Neither can I." She lay back on the pillow and stared at the ceiling.

Lucas sensed a wavering in the flame of her fire. It chilled him. Words formed that he knew must be said, yet he feared the answer. *Do I dare ask?*

"Victoria? Are you having second thoughts about us? Is that what kept you awake?"

She hesitated. "Knowing who Rayen is changes everything and nothing."

He shivered. She tucked the covers around them.

"I love you, Lucas, and I can't wait to be your wife. That hasn't and will never change. Your daughter has been through an ordeal that I can't begin to wrap my head around. If who she is and how we'll adjust to that kept us awake, think about her struggle. She thought you knew. You didn't. She may have considered the possibility that you met another woman, got married, and had a family. Or she may have refused to let herself go there. Whether she did or not, I am that reality." She reached for and squeezed his hand. "Rayen needs us. But she'll need more than we can give her to help process the past and move on."

Lucas gathered her in his arms and held her. He kissed places where her favored fragrance lingered. Lightly caressed her cheeks and lips with his fingertips. "You are wise, mon amour."

Her fingers twirled the hair on his chest. "I don't know about that. But I do know I'm hungry. And I smell coffee. I guess one or both of our hosts couldn't sleep either."

"Maybe they're early risers."

"I don't think so. You know I am. Whenever I called Kelly before I left for work, I could tell from her voice that she wasn't awake. I know I woke Eddie up more than once." Tori tossed back the duvet and sat up on the side of the bed. "Now, where did I leave that robe?"

Lucas followed her movements in first light of day shadows. The curve of her. The subtle grace in her. He felt the fire burn that only she could ignite in him. "Victoria." He patted the down-filled tufts with his palm and held out his arms to her.

She went to him. Held his hands in hers. "Lucas," she sighed and lay back with him on the bed.

He kissed her. Savored her. Lovingly touched all that he admired and adored about her. She gave all she had to him and, with him, whispered a promise of love for their lifetime.

Chapter 49

The Morning After

Kelly poured the last of the coffee in the carafe into her cup. "Running on empty."

"I'm on it, babe." Steam pumped and hissed from the drip coffee side of Eddie's prized barista-grade machine. A buttery croissant on the large tray of assorted pastries caught his eye. He slid a plate from the stack next to the goodies on the kitchen island's marble top and settled onto the swivel seat of the stool across from hers. "How long have you been up?" he asked her. "Long enough to order up a mother lode of calories, I see."

"We have guests. I woke up and gave up on sleep after the second, or was it the third time I thought you were talking to me."

"Sorry. I was replaying last night in my head."

"No lie." She plopped a chocolate-iced donut with particolored sprinkles on her plate.

Eddie ate half of his croissant and got up to refill the carafe. "You don't eat donuts."

"When I'm sleep deprived, I need all the sugar and caffeine I can get."

"Me, too." Tori padded in on borrowed slippers. A fluffy robe covered clothes she'd worn the day before. "That coffee smells incredible."

"Jamaican Blue Mountain. Finest kind." Eddie poured and set a full cup in front of her. "Good morning."

"Yes, it is, after an awful night." Tori sat on the stool beside Kelly and wrapped her hands around the white china warmth. "Thank God we're all here, safe and in one piece."

"How did you sleep?" Kelly asked.

"Not great. Dozed mostly. Rayen fell asleep as soon as her head hit the pillow."

"Is Lucas asleep?" Kelly asked.

"No, he's checking on his daughter." Kelly couldn't tell if Tori winced from the burn of sipped coffee or the words that had just tumbled off her tongue. "That is going to take some getting used to."

"I probably shouldn't ask this, but," Kelly started to say.

"Is Rayen telling the truth?" Tori finished the thought for her. "Probably. Lucas is certain Adriana left Canada with her mother in May. Rayen was born in December. She told Lucas that when her grandmother found out her daughter was pregnant, the family married Adriana off to this Vasquez guy. Rayen grew up believing that he was her father. And he was bad to the bone. Abused and used both of them like property. Rayen earned her keep hustling tourists on the streets. Neither of us was brave enough to ask what Vasquez forced on Adriana."

"Did Rayen say when and why she left Buenos Aires?" Eddie asked.

Tori swallowed a mouthful of coffee and nodded. "Vasquez started running guns and drugs across South American and eventually international borders about ten years ago. Then he got involved in human trafficking. Adriana hoarded whatever cash she could and gave her daughter what she had to send her to the only safe place she knew. That's when she told Rayen about Lucas and where to find him. She begged her mother to go with her. But Adriana refused. There wasn't enough money for the two of them to survive, and Adriana was afraid if they both left Vasquez would come after them. Rayen got as far as St. Louis when the money ran out. She hitched a ride with a recruiter who promised to get her a job in Chicago. She's been more or less a slave to Otto Hermann for the last six or seven years."

"My God," Eddie shook his head. "All that evil happening every day right under our noses."

The phone's ring interrupted their thoughts and moments of silence. "I'll get it," Eddie said. "That's gotta be Jim."

***

Lucas stood in the doorway of the room Rayen had chosen. Sheer curtains diffused sunlight that could have been blocked out by closing the heavier draperies. She'd insisted the door be left open and the light be let in.

My daughter, he thought. She lay on her back, burrowed in comfort on the king-sized bed under linens, blankets, and a duvet, with her head resting on plump pillows. Cassie nestled at her feet, a snoring ball of fur tipped by a wet nose and stumpy tail.

She stirred at the trill of the phone in the hallway. "Papa."

He went to her. Sat beside her on the bed. Flinched at the greenish-blue stains of violence on her cheekbone. "Buenos dias, Rayen."

Her eyelids fluttered. "Do I have to get up now?"

"Not if you don't want to."

The corners of her mouth lifted to a contented smile. "This is so nice." She closed her eyes. "I haven't slept in a proper bed in so long."

Regret over years lost and the suffering she could have been spared stung him. *Why didn't you tell me, Adriana? I would have found a way to bring you and our daughter home!* "Go back to sleep, my dear one." He kissed her forehead and rose slowly to his feet. He scratched Cassie behind her ears on his way out. "Look after her, little one." Lucas turned back at the doorway. *My daughter.* He left the door open.

186

Chapter 50

Scars

Jim thanked the doorman, who didn't ask to see his badge. "Good to see you again, Ms. Vosh." He winked at Cecily. She winked back.

"Someone's a frequent flyer." Jim draped his arm around her shoulders and headed for the elevator.

Cecily poked his ribs through wintertime layers. "Is someone jealous?"

"Not yet. But I could get there." Jim waited for the doors to close and kissed her with an urgency for the intimacy he hadn't felt in years.

"Didn't get enough last night?" she teased.

"At my age, a man's gotta keep the engines running. Can't let 'em cool down." He nibbled her ear and whispered in it. "What do you want with an old war horse like me?"

"Everything you've got and more of it."

Their lips locked. The doors opened.

Eddie cleared his throat. "OK. This I did not expect to see. Need a moment? A room?"

"Funny. Ha ha." Jim wiped his lips on the cuff of his coat sleeve. "Always the jokester." He stepped back and held out his hand for Cecily. "After you, Ms. Vosh."

Cecily pursed her mouth in a self-satisfied smile. "Thank you, Detective Ross." She passed Eddie and joined Kelly and their guests in the front room with a Magnificent Mile and Great Lake view.

"Well, folks, I need statements." Jim took off his coat and plopped in the largest leather armchair. "Paul took Cecily's at the station house this morning. He and I have written up our reports. Frankly, all we need to do is fill in the blanks with your sides of the story. Especially yours," he looked at Lucas, "and if I heard Eddie right, your daughter's."

Lucas sat next to Tori on the edge of the sectional cushion. Feet flat on the floor. Elbows on his knees. Palms up and open. "Detective, I am happy to answer all of your questions. You heard correctly. Rayen is my daughter. I was not aware until last night. Eddie told me that you also have a daughter. Please, I ask you as a father. She needs time to ..."

"I will talk to the police, Papa." Everyone turned to look at the young woman whose plight had connected them. Rayen stood tall and proud, shoulders back, head held high. Her tattered clothing was discarded and replaced by gray wool slacks and an ivory cashmere sweater from Kelly's surplus in the guest room closet. Her eyes shone with a determined inner strength. She walked in on black ballerina slippers and sat on the sofa beside her father. "You said that he would not hurt me again. I must do what I can to ensure he will never hurt or kill anyone else."

"Good." Jim nodded. "Very good." He fished the digital recorder and smartphone backup in his coat pocket. "We need a room, Eddie." His raised eyebrow dared Eddie to keep it professional.

"You can use my office," Eddie said. He led them past the elevator to the opposite side of the penthouse.

***

Quiet descended in the wide-open space arranged for comfort, alarmed for security, and bathed in December afternoon sunlight.

"Well, Cec, I guess you've got nothing left to say, and our interrogation is on hold for now, Tori," Kelly said. "I'll make more coffee."

Cecily touched her friend's knee. "That can wait." She scooted closer to Kelly, so close that their knees touched. "I've had all the pieces for months now. Comparing notes with Jim and Paul put the puzzle together. I wasn't sure how or when to tell you, but this is as good a time as any." She took a breath. "It's about your brother."

Tori shifted on the couch cushion. "You have a brother?" she asked Kelly.

"Had a brother," Kelly replied. "I told you he ... died."

Tori hesitated. "I don't remember having that conversation."

"Well, maybe we did. Maybe we didn't." Kelly looked at Cecily. "I thought we agreed not to pursue this anymore."

"I didn't agree to that. I couldn't. I promised you I would find out who killed Caleb."

"Whoa!" Tori's eyes widened and rolled. "Now I know you never mentioned your brother. I think I should find somewhere else to be."

"No!" Kelly's raised voice startled both women. "You're a guest in our home, Tori, and we are not going to talk about that now, Cec."

Kelly started to get up. Cecily's fingers circled her friend's wrist. "Kelly, your brother was not the saint you thought he was. Otto Hermann murdered him because Caleb cheated him."

"You're lying!" Kelly pulled her hand away from Cecily's grasp.

"It's all in here." Cecily held up her cell phone. "The police reports, names, photos, evidence list. Hermann needed a clean-cut, All-American young Caucasian male to run drugs for him after police profiling rounded up his Latino connections. Caleb fit the bill. But he made a big mistake. He underestimated Hermann's contempt for liars and anyone who dared to steal from him. It cost him his life."

Kelly's eyes narrowed. Her face contorted in anger. "I don't believe you."

"Then look!" Cecily grabbed Kelly's hand and shoved the phone into her open palm. "See for yourself!"

Kelly dropped the phone to the carpet as though touching it burned her. "I will not!" She got up and paced the wall of windows, away from the facts that shattered her truth.

Cecily picked up her discarded phone. "You've got to let him go, Kelly. You have got to move on for your sake and Eddie's."

Kelly turned her back and physically distanced herself from the facts that shattered her truth. She paced the wall of windows. Her shoulders shook.

Tori tugged at and twirled a curl through her fingers. "Shouldn't you go and talk to her?" she asked.

Cecily shook her head and sighed. "It wouldn't do any good. She won't listen. Kelly has to work it out. She'll talk when she's ready."

"How long have you known Kelly?" Tori asked.

"Since her brother's murder. It was my first homicide investigation as a rookie detective. Caleb was only eighteen. The family was over the top distraught. I went to his funeral. The room was packed with people and flowers. A framed family photo was on an easel next to his closed coffin. I remember Kelly and her mom and dad standing next to it, hanging on to each other like they were afraid to let go. They thought Caleb had been killed for his car. I always thought there was more to it than that. I pulled double shifts. Worked on my days off. I tried so hard to solve that case even after it was tossed on the cold as ice pile." Cecily sat back down and rested her stocking feet on the ottoman.

"Does she have other siblings? What about her parents?"

"It was just Kelly and Caleb. Her dad didn't live long after his son's death. Natural causes. I think he died of a broken heart. Her mom faded away. Dementia. Forgetting took away her pain."

"That is so sad." Tori's frown lifted slightly. "But she has Eddie. Won't they be getting married soon?"

"You'd think. They've been friends since college and in love for years before they admitted it. But something is stopping them. I thought it was Kelly not knowing about Caleb. I hoped if I found out the who and why of how he died, that would close the wound on that scar." Cecily sat up and dropped her head in her hands. "I shouldn't be telling you all this."

Tori stopped twirling her curl and snapped her fingers. "Maybe you should. You and Kelly have too much history. Maybe she'll talk to me." Tori walked to the windows and stood beside a now stationary Kelly. They stared out at the slice of the city below and people in motion on the street, sidewalks, and paths that curved along the lake shore. "I was afraid of my scar."

Kelly stopped staring and turned her head toward Tori. "Excuse me?"

"I found the lump and thought for sure I had breast cancer. I was so scared that I didn't go to the doctor immediately, which was dumb. The lump got bigger. The biopsy was inconclusive. So, I had surgery. I was lucky. I didn't have cancer. But I did have a scar that I didn't want anyone to see. I saw that scar as a total sexual turn-off. Then I met Lucas. I wanted him so much. But I was afraid of my scar. Do you know what he said to me?" Tori looked at Kelly. "He said, 'Victoria, we all have scars. Some we can see. Others we hold inside.'

I realized then that I had more than one scar. One on my breast and another in my head. When I let go of that fear, the scar on the outside didn't matter anymore."

Kelly's gaze returned to the dazzling panorama. "I suppose Cecily told you about my brother."

"And your mom and dad. Your scar got wider and deeper with every loss."

"And every disappointment, including my two failed marriages."

"Oh, I'm sorry. I didn't know about those." Tori put her arm around Kelly. "Have you told Eddie?"

"He knows about my exes."

"But not about your brother and your parents."

"He knows Caleb and Dad are dead. That's it. No details."

"Kelly, Eddie can't see your scar. You're holding that inside. You love him. Why are you afraid to tell him?"

Kelly caught the gathering tears with her fingertips. "I don't know. Maybe because he has a family and I don't."

"But you do," Tori told her. "You have each other."

Kelly hugged Tori and let the tears flow freely for the love and family she'd lost.

Chapter 51

Devastating News

J im filled the recorder with abbreviated statements from Kelly and Tori. Satisfied, he gathered up his equipment and slipped into his coat. "Well, that does it for now," he said. "Don't take any long trips anytime soon. Oh, about that. Any idea when your government will call you back, Lucas?"

"There are concerns for my safety. The request was that I return immediately," Lucas said. "But Rayen insists on staying here to testify for the prosecution. This morning, I told the Consulate General that I would not leave without Rayen. We will be relocated to a more secure apartment closer to the consulate."

"You're welcome to stay here as long as you want or need to," Eddie said.

"We appreciate that very much, my friend," Lucas said. "Thank you. I do need to pick up my car."

"And I need to go to my apartment and get some clean clothes," Tori said.

"I'd like to come with you, Papa," Rayen said.

"I can drop you folks off at Two Pru if you don't mind riding in an unmarked," Jim offered.

Hearing no objections, Lucas agreed and thanked Jim. "I've been meaning to ask you, detective. How is the undercover officer injured by the man Rayen knew as Dragon?"

"You mean Perez," Jim confirmed. Lucas nodded. "He's still in the hospital. But he is recovering. Should be released any day now."

"Rayen was afraid that he was me. I'd like to visit him. Thank him for what he tried to do," Lucas said.

Jim grinned. "I think that could be arranged." Cecily walked alongside him to the elevator. "Not that I minded," Jim said to her, "but why did you follow me here from the station house? You got your car out of lockup. You could have gone back home."

"I wanted to tell Kelly about her brother before I lost my nerve."

"How did that go?"

"She shut me out. Tori did get Kelly to talk to her. I'm not sure what was said. But I sure hope my stubborn mule friend talks to Eddie." Cecily slid her arm under Jim's coat and squeezed his backside. "Keep that engine running."

***

The ringtone notes of the Canadian national anthem woke Lucas's cell phone midway along the short trip to Two Prudential Plaza. "Oui, allo," he answered and carried on the brief conversation in French.

Tori reacted to his frown. "Something wrong, love?" she asked.

"Inspector Freeland and Agent Cartier are with the Consulate General. They want to talk with me and with Rayen. I told them we're on our way, and you are with us."

"I suppose I can catch a cab to my apartment and wait for you there."

"No, Victoria. Whatever they have to say, you should hear it, too." Lucas thanked Jim at the curb and guided Tori and Rayen from the revolving doors at street level to Suite 2400. The Canadian officers were waiting for them in Lucas's office.

Agent Cartier glanced at Tori. She looked at Lucas. "Sir, the information we have is sensitive and confidential."

"Victoria is my fiancée soon to be my wife and a permanent resident of Canada." He arranged a trio of chairs in the center of the room and sat between Tori and Rayen.

Donald Freeland and Lea Cartier exchanged looks. "Very well," the CSIS agent said. She rolled out the remaining chair from a corner conference table

193

and sat facing their circle, her legs crossed at the knees and hands folded in her lap. The RCMP officer stood beside her. His stiff stance and stern expression increased the tension.

"Sir, CSIS has determined the identity of the man you met with in Buenos Aires who had intercepted the money order sent from the bodega in Chicago. He is an international agent employed by Central and South American governments and the U.S. to identify and track contraband smuggling operations. Luis Vasquez is, or rather was, a suspect of interest in ongoing investigations across several borders and two continents. This agent has confirmed Vasquez is in prison in Colombia. But not for smuggling." Agent Cartier paused. Her hard professional edges softened. Her shoulders curved. Her hands unfolded. "He was convicted for the murder of his wife. I am so sorry."

Lucas clenched his fists. His arms trembled. Pain radiated from every pore and nerve in his body. "Adriana." He moaned her name from the depths of his soul and closed his eyes.

The sob that shook Rayen rose from the core of her being, the agony of a child ripped from her mother's arms. "Mama!" She slumped and swayed on the edge of the chair.

Tori dropped to her knees between them. She caught and embraced her family to break their fall.

Chapter 52

Change of Heart

Outside, the cooler hue of the late December sun transitioned to lavender twilight. Inside, the penthouse glistened with the colors of the season. Crystal ornaments on a genuine Noble fir tree glowed in the light of golden LED strands. Tiny red lights twined in pine branches, and sprigs of holly hung by a hired team of decorators, blinked and winked with the advent of evening.

"That croissant is sitting like a brick in my belly." Eddie tried to fill the sudden silence with small talk that Kelly seemed not to hear. He stopped tidying up the kitchen when she didn't respond. "Any ideas on what we'll serve our guests for dinner?" Eddie moved and stood between Kelly and the hypnotic natural gas-fueled flame dance in the fireplace. "We could go out. But my personal preference is a quiet night in. What's your vote?"

Kelly seemed to stare right through him.

I'm talking to myself. It's like I'm not here. He tried again with a conversation starter he was certain she couldn't ignore. "Jim and Cecily were lip-locked and groping each other in the elevator."

No reaction. *What the unbelievable hell.*

"Look, if you're not going to talk to me, I might as well go for an early run."

When she looked up at him, the hurt in her swollen and bloodshot eyes startled him to the brink of fright. "Babe." He sat beside her. Her hand he touched was cold. "What's wrong? Are you thinking about last night? Yeah, it was scary. But it all turned out OK."

She shook her head. "We've been through worse."

"Then what is it?"

She laced her fingers through his and squeezed. "You've told me everything about your family. I met your father and not under the best of circumstances."

Eddie grinned and kissed her cheek. "You covered by a robe standing in the middle of his bedroom suite with your hair in a towel. Have to admit I'd never seen Edward, the Elder, so flustered."

Kelly grinned back at him. "That afternoon, we were in Ruby's kitchen when I said it reminded me of my grandma's. I know you were kidding about not knowing I had a grandmother. But I realized then that I've never told you about my family in all the years we've known each other. My life before we met." She breathed in the fresh scent of the season around them and sighed. "It's about time I did."

Her story spooled out like thread from a coiled bobbin unwound. The cookie cutters and fascinating gadgets her grandmother used to make sugary treats and savory biscuits in that kitchen. Her whimsical salt and pepper shakers shaped like roosters, and a Dutch boy and girl in wooden shoes.

The songs her mother hummed while ironing her father's white dress shirts every Saturday afternoon. Saturday nights watching British sitcoms and wearing sparkly fake stone necklaces with matching clip-on earrings from her mother's jewelry box. Sundays spent reading the paper with Dad and playing word games he made up to help her learn spelling and grammar.

She shared precious memories of the cherubic face that masked the imp within her brother Caleb. He'd annoyed her when she missed the bus searching for the book bag he'd hidden. Angered her when he left with his friends on the nights he was supposed to clear and wash the dinner dishes. Made her laugh with his overblown imitation of the pompous English teacher who marked the best essay she'd ever written with a big red B and promised revenge when a lie threatened to tear her adolescent world apart.

His darker side had killed him. Eddie listened as the black curtain descended on Chicago and Kelly's story. Her father's heart was stopped by grief he couldn't bear. Her mother still living but no longer self-aware. Cecily's resolve to reveal the how, why, and who of Caleb's violent death and the bombshell of truth she'd dropped that afternoon.

"I love you, Eddie, and I want to marry you. I couldn't figure out why I put off setting a date. I knew it wasn't because of my two previous mistakes. They happened because I really wanted you, but I didn't think you wanted me in that way, and I didn't want to screw up our friendship so …"

"We've already crossed and burned that bridge." His arm circled her shoulders. "You've been dragging around a load of dirty laundry that Cecily cracked opened and dumped out." He softly squeezed her arm and kissed her lips. "I get it, Kel. I really do. This is all too much. So take as much time as you need. I'd marry you tomorrow if you said the word. But I can wait."

"Maybe I don't want to anymore. It's totally stupid to delay getting on with our lives because of a lie I believed and a hurt I couldn't help. My family is gone. But I'm not alone. We have each other." Kelly snuggled under Eddie's arm. "Tell me about your brothers."

Eddie grinned. "Nathaniel, don't call him Nate, and Bartholomew, always call him Bart. They are total opposites. Nathaniel's pants have to be pressed with a perfect crease. He never wears jeans or a shirt without a tie. His grammar is precise, and he won't say shit with a mouthful. Bart breaks out in a rash when he wears a suit, lives in jeans, and swears like a sailor."

Kelly laughed out loud. "And what about your sister Cassandra, right?"

His grin stretched to a smile. "She's a sweetheart. She throws herself into everything she does. Hugging trees, homeless dogs, and the kids Cassie reads stories to at the library where she works. She's the opposite of our mother. There's nothing pretentious or phony about Cassie."

At the mention of her name, Tori's dog opened her eyes and thumped her tail on the cushion where she'd curled up next to Kelly. She ruffled the dog's fur. "Don't get too comfortable, kid. You'll be Canadian soon." Kelly leaned in and looked up at Eddie. "How soon can your mother plan a wedding?"

Eddie's jaw dropped. "You're joking, right?"

"Just answer the question."

"Felicity is a born event planner. All she needs is a guest list and seventy-two hours."

"Would you object to our getting married in Connecticut?"

"I'll marry you anywhere. But why Connecticut?"

I want a fresh start, a world away from the pain. "Well, your family is there. And at the risk of sounding shallow or greedy," *Oh, what the hell!* "I want a real wedding with more flowers than a botanical center and a cake so big, we'd need a ladder to reach the top. I want a dress to swoon over. I want to hire a famous photographer known for work that hangs in galleries. I want to dance to live music and not give a damn how much it all costs." Kelly sat up straight and turned to him. "I've been married twice in city halls. No cake. No dress. No flowers. No photos. No one around to celebrate what should have been a happy occasion because it wasn't real." She took his hands in hers. "What we have is real, Eddie. I want to celebrate our love and new life with your family and my new family around us."

Eddie stroked her hair and touched his forehead with hers. "I love you, Kelly. So will my family and the invited elite of Bridgeport on my mother's guest list."

Their shoulders shook with laughter. "OK, Sherlock." Kelly swatted his knee with her palm. "Let's set a date."

Cassie barked her approval.

Chapter 53

New Beginnings

The deep freeze of January dissolved with the slushy respite of a Groundhog Day thaw and Punxsutawney Phil's prediction of an early spring. Eddie and Kelly put the agency on voicemail hold until after their Valentine's Day wedding and return from a honeymoon destination Eddie kept secret.

"Aw, look." Kelly held up her cell phone. "Tori posted photos from their wedding." She flipped through images of the civil ceremony and private reception held in the Art Institute gallery where Tori and Lucas met. "This one is my favorite." The photo framed Rayen cradling Tori's cascading bouquet of pink stargazer lilies and red roses as a jubilant Lucas kissed his radiant bride. The joy in his daughter's smile was genuine.

"I was surprised when we got the invitation," Eddie said. "I thought they were going to wait and get married in Montreal. Probably was for the best, though. Jim says the internal affairs investigation of the trail De Leon tracked through at least two station houses could hold up Hermann's trial for months."

"I think the three of them needed something to celebrate," Kelly said.

"Weddings will do that." Eddie shrugged his shoulders into a lighter-weight coat than usual for mid-February.

"Where are you going?" she demanded. "In case you've forgotten, the flight taking us to our wedding leaves in sixteen hours."

"It's a private jet, Kel. The pilot won't take off without us." He kissed her and rattled the MG's keys in his pocket. "Petula is calling to me. We'll be back before dinner."

**

Eddie had helped the artisan jeweler move into her shop on the ground floor of the Lake Bluff building where The UnMatchables opened for business. He'd been impressed with the uniqueness of her work. He told her about Kelly, how she'd saved him from self-destruction, their friendship, business partnership, and at long last upcoming marriage. He'd asked her to design a piece of wearable art for him to give his wife on their wedding night.

Tumblers clicked to open the office safe installed by a previous tenant. Kelly knew it was there but didn't use it or ask him for the combination. Eddie lifted the lid on the dark blue velvet box in his hand. Each intricate link in the delicate tri-color precious metal weave of the bracelet told their story. *It's perfect and perfectly Kelly.* He closed the safe and flipped off the overhead lights on his way out. Eddie pivoted on the hallway side of the locked door and stepped on the toes of wing-tipped shoes in desperate need of a shine.

"Eddie Emerson?" The wild-eyed owner in the shoes took a step back.

"Yeah." *Who the hell is this?* "Can I help you?"

A middle-aged man with a ragged beard over splotched ruddy skin waved a paperback copy of Eddie's twelfth or was it his thirteenth, true crime novel, in the author's face. "You lied about me in this book. You've got to rewrite it. Set the record straight. I need you to tell the truth!"

Eddie jotted a quick mental note of the rumpled threadbare brown with white pinstripe suit. No amount of bleach would whiten the set-in stain on his shirt. The knot of his paisley-patterned tie lay sideways over his collarbone. He needed a shave, and his breath reeked of garlic and cigars.

"Buddy, I don't remember the details of this particular case. I don't know who you are, and right now I don't have time to find out."

"Please!" The man tried to block Eddie's exit. "I'm ruined! You've got to fix the damage you did!"

"Look." Eddie patted his pockets and found a small stash of business cards. He pressed one into the man's palm. "I've gotta go. Give me a call in four weeks. Make an appointment." He headed for and down the staircase.

The setting sun cast long shadows across the hardwood entryway. Eddie didn't want to look back or up, but he did. The disheveled man stood and stared at The UnMatchables office door. He wasn't wearing a coat.

THE END

Afterword

Hidden in Plain Sight

Faces frozen in time lost to human trafficking stare back at us from paper pinned to bulletin boards and taped on public washroom stall doors. Abbreviated stories of missing person misery are reported in print and captured in video documentaries.

According to an International Labour Organization report published in 2022 there are 27.6 million people in forced labour situations on any given day. Forced labour, as set out in the ILO Forced Labour Convention, 1930, refers to "all work or service which is exacted from any person under the menace of any penalty and for which the said person has not offered himself voluntarily."

Traffickers prey on people of all ages, backgrounds, and nationalities, exploiting them for their own profit. Women and girls make up 11.8 million of the total. More than 3.3 million are children.

The share of migrant workers in forced labour is more than three times higher than the number of non-migrant workers in the overall labour force." (International Labour Organization, 2022)

In the United States, traffickers compel victims to engage in commercial sex and to work in both legal and illicit industries and sectors, including peddling and begging, drug smuggling and distribution, and domestic work. (US Department of State, 2023)

Statistics Canada states 2278 victims of human traffickers were reported to and by police from 2010-2020; 95% of the victims were women and girls and nearly half were under the age of 25. (Statistics Canada, 2023)

The Dirty War

The military junta that ruled Argentina from 1976 to 1983 silenced dissidents through the arbitrary detention, torture and unlawful killing of dozens of people at a secret detention centre set up in a military school in Buenos Aires. Many of the 30,000 who "disappeared" have never been found.

In October 2011, a court in Buenos Aires convicted 16 former military officials for crimes against humanity. More than 150 witnesses testified including 80 survivors of The Dirty War. (Amnesty International, 2011)

About The Author

Teresa LaBella grew up in Davenport, Iowa where the Mississippi River runs east to west. She holds a BA in Mass Communication from St. Ambrose University in Iowa, and an MA in Community Arts Management from University of Illinois.

The people she interviewed as a journalist and met in her work in the arts and other nonprofit organizations coloured her future fiction writing canvas and sharpened her love for telling a good story. A member of the Writers' Federation of Nova Scotia, Teresa resides in rural Nova Scotia, Canada with her rescued fur babies Rosie and Ellis.

Connect with Teresa LaBella

www.storyteller30.com
Facebook.com/storyteller30
Goodreads.com/author/show/7792630.Teresa_LaBella
Bookbub.com/authors/teresa-labella

Author's Note

Dear Readers,

Whether you downloaded the story on your e-reader, added a paperback copy to your shelf or borrowed the book from your local library—thank you!

Please take the time to help others discover *Danger Revealed*. Consider posting a review on Goodreads and Amazon and recommending the novel to your book club, family, neighbors, and friends.

If you loved *Danger Revealed* then you won't want to miss *Capital Ties*, a political thriller! Lucas, Tori and Rayen return in *Capital Ties*, a uniquely Canadian tale of intrigue set in Ottawa, the shifting epicenter of political power plays and dangerous players.

I look forward to connecting with you and reading your reviews!

Warm wishes,

Teresa

Works Cited

Amnesty International. (2011, October 27). Retrieved from Amnesty International:https://www.amnesty.org/en/latest/news/2011/10/argentina convicts-former-military-officials-edirty-ware-crimes/

International Labour Organization. (2022, September 12). Ilo.org. Retrieved from International Labour Organization: https://www.ilo.org/global/topics/forced-labour/lang--en/index.htm

Shana Conroy and Danielle Sutton. (2023, June 9). Retrieved from Statistics Canada: https://www150.statcan.gc.ca/n1/pub/85002x/2022001/article/00010eng.htm

US Department of State. (2023). Retrieved from US Department of State: https://www.state.gov/humantrafficking-about-human trafficking/#:~:text=This%20report%20also%20estimates%20that